Recorder
My First
Music

Easy to Read • Easy to Use
Beginners to Intermediate

Roger Cawkwell

FLAME TREE
PUBLISHING

Publisher & Creative Director: Nick Wells
Editor: Polly Prior
Designer: Jake

Special thanks to: Peter Booth (Early Music Shop), Cat Taylor

09 11 13 12 10

1 3 5 7 9 10 8 6 4 2

This edition first published 2009 by
FLAME TREE PUBLISHING
Crabtree Hall, Crabtree Lane
Fulham, London, SW6 6TY
United Kingdom
www.flametreepublishing.com

Flame Tree Publishing is part of the
Foundry Creative Media Company Limited

Roger Cawkwell studied composition, piano, sax, flute and clarinet at the
Royal Academy of Music, leaving in the early 1970s to go on to play with the
John Dankworth Band and the London Sinfonietta. He has always been
active as a teacher, currently running musicianship classes at Goldsmiths
College, London, and has contributed to several music educational projects.
As well as adding recorder to the other woodwinds, Roger has gone on to
learn many instruments and now plays most of the brass family, too.

ISBN 978-1-84786-656-1

Printed in China

Contents

Contents

Introduction

This book will introduce young players and other beginners to the recorder and will also include an explanation of the basics of music notation and theory. All of the musical examples and fingering charts are for the descant or soprano recorder, which is the type most frequently used to begin with.

As you will see a few pages further on there is a whole family of recorders, from the tiny sopranino to the enormous bass and contrabass recorders; many recorder players may eventually learn to play several different sizes, but most will start right here with the descant.

Getting
Started

B,A,G

C&D

F#,E,D

Bb&F

Low C
& C#

High
E-G

G#
& D#

Songbook
ONE

Songbook
TWO

Songbook
THREE

Songbook
FOUR

Getting Started

Before you start playing notes or tunes, you need to get to know the recorder itself. The first section of the book looks at how the recorder works, introduces you to some other members of the recorder family, and shows you how to hold, blow and care for your instrument.

It also contains some easy bits of music theory, which will help you when you come the first tunes later in the book.

We introduce you to the Fingering Chart as well, which is used throughout the book to show you how to play all the notes you need to learn.

Happy playing!

B,A,G

C&D

F#,E,D

Bb&F

Low C
& C#

High
E–G

G#
& D#

Songbook
ONE

Songbook
TWO

Songbook
THREE

Songbook
FOUR

Getting
Started

B,A,G

C&D

F#,E,D

Bb&F

Low C
& C#

High
E-G

G#
& D#

Songbook
ONE

Songbook
TWO

Songbook
THREE

Songbook
FOUR

What Is A Recorder?

The recorder is a pipe with a mouthpiece at one end. It can be made from plastic or wood.

Fipple

The recorder has a little window towards the top of it, called a **fipple**. When you blow into the mouthpiece, your breath strikes against a

Getting
Started

B,A,G

C&D

F#,E,D

Bb&F

Low C
& C#

High
E-G

G#
& D#

Songbook
ONE

Songbook
TWO

Songbook
THREE

Songbook
FOUR

sharp edge in the fipple. Some of the air goes out of the instrument and some goes inside it, creating a whistling sound.

Playing Notes

The sound goes down the main body of the instrument, which is a tube with holes in it. When you put your fingers on the holes, you close off different lengths of the tube. The tube tunes the sound to definite musical notes. Even though it is a very simple instrument, the recorder can play all of the notes you need to play music.

Getting
Started

B,A,G

C&D

F#,E,D

Bb&F

Low C
& C#

High
E-G

G#
& D#

Songbook
ONE

Songbook
TWO

Songbook
THREE

Songbook
FOUR

Parts Of The Recorder

Almost all soprano/descant recorders come in three parts: the headpiece, the main body and the foot joint. The photograph here shows the main parts. Have a look at yours to see how it fits all together.

The headpiece is fitted onto the larger end of the main body with a gentle twisting action so that the window is in line with the row of six holes.

The foot joint fits on the smaller end. Turn it so that you can easily reach the holes with your right little finger.

Getting Started

B,A,G

C&D

F#,E,D

Bb&F

Low C & C#

High E-G

G# & D#

Songbook ONE

Songbook TWO

Songbook THREE

Songbook FOUR

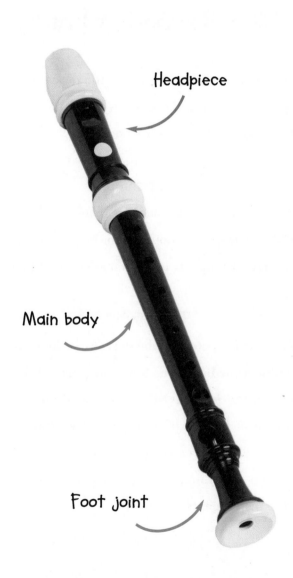

Headpiece

Main body

Foot joint

Getting
Started

B,A,G

C♦D

F#,E,D

Bb♦F

Low C
♦ C#

High
E-G

G#
♦ D#

Songbook
ONE

Songbook
TWO

Songbook
THREE

Songbook
FOUR

The Recorder Family

When you have begun to play the descant/ soprano recorder, there is a whole family of similar instruments for you to try.

Sopranino

The sopranino is the smallest member of the family, being only about 24 cm long, and plays the highest notes. It is often made in one piece.

Treble/Alto

The next largest after the descant is the treble or alto recorder. It has the same parts as the descant but is about 48 cm long. Sopranino and treble have a different way of writing the notes for any given fingering, so be prepared to learn something new when you move to these instruments.

Tenor

The tenor recorder is bigger still at about 62 cm. Being twice the length of the descant it sounds a whole octave lower for any given fingering but is too large for small hands, even though the right little finger sometimes has a key to help it cover the lowest hole.

Getting Started

B,A,G

C&D

F#,E,D

Bb&F

Low C & C#

High E-G

G# & D#

Songbook ONE

Songbook TWO

Songbook THREE

Songbook FOUR

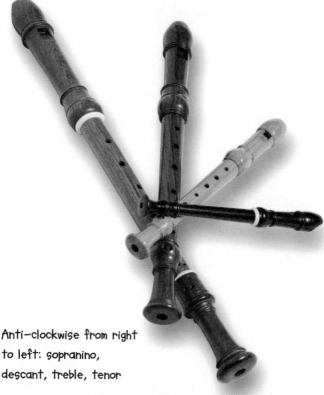

Anti-clockwise from right to left: sopranino, descant, treble, tenor

Bass ♦ Contra–Bass

You would need really large hands to play the bass or contra-bass. These instruments are so big they are either supported on a sling or rest on the floor.

Bass recorder

Their music is usually written in the bass clef (which we're not going to cover in this book) so there will be something new to learn here, too.

B,A,G

C&D

F#,E,D

Bb&F

Low C
& C#

High
E-G

G#
& D#

Songbook
ONE

Songbook
TWO

Songbook
THREE

Songbook
FOUR

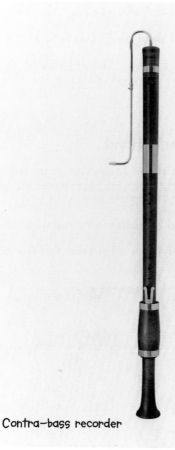

Contra-bass recorder

Getting
Started

B,A,G

C♶D

F♯,E,D

Bb♶F

Low C
♶ C♯

High
E–G

G♯
♶ D♯

Songbook
ONE

Songbook
TWO

Songbook
THREE

Songbook
FOUR

How Should I Hold The Recorder?

The recorder should be held very lightly. You may be frightened of dropping it at first but if you clutch it too tightly your fingers will be too stiff to play well.

Left Hand

The thumb and first three fingers of your left hand are needed for fingering notes, so you shouldn't use them to hold the instrument. Don't try to support the recorder with your left thumb.

Right Hand

Your right thumb provides support, along with your mouth, as you blow into the instrument. Only touch the instrument with your other right hand fingers when you play notes.

Three-Point Hold

Place the recorder to your lips (not into your mouth!) with your right thumb under the body and with your left middle finger covering the second hole (see the picture). You can try playing a note if you like.

This will give you the three-point hold: lips, right thumb and one or more fingers on a hole.

Getting
Started

B,A,G

C&D

F#,E,D

Bb&F

Low C
& C#

High
E-G

G#
& D#

Songbook
ONE

Songbook
TWO

Songbook
THREE

Songbook
FOUR

Getting
Started

B,A,G

C&D

F#,E,D

Bb&F

Low C
& C#

High
E-G

G#
& D#

Songbook
ONE

Songbook
TWO

Songbook
THREE

Songbook
FOUR

How Should I Blow
The Recorder?

Do not put the recorder into your mouth like a clarinet or saxophone. Instead, put the recorder to your lips, with your lips just far enough apart to let some air through.

Breath Control

Blow a steady, gentle stream of air into the recorder and you should hear a steady, musical tone. If you blow too hard you get a shriek, too softly and you will get a whistly, wavery sound. This may seem simple but it is quite hard to do evenly and is one of the main secrets of good recorder playing.

Musicians call this 'breath control' and take it very seriously, so you might as well learn about it right from the start.

Getting Started

B,A,G

C&D

F#,E,D

Bb&F

Low C & C#

High E-G

G# & D#

Songbook ONE

Songbook TWO

Songbook THREE

Songbook FOUR

Getting
Started

B,A,G

C&D

F#,E,D

Bb&F

Low C
& C#

High
E-G

G#
& D#

Songbook
ONE

Songbook
TWO

Songbook
THREE

Songbook
FOUR

Practice Makes Perfect

To get really good at breath control, start each practice session by blowing into just the headpiece. Try to play the notes evenly, without wobbles or bumps, and for as long as you can. This may seem hard at first but it is a skill you must learn, bit by bit, if you are to make a nice sound on the recorder.

This exercise is not exciting, but it is important. Try and keep doing it, even if for just a minute, before you put the rest of your recorder together and start playing some tunes.

How would you draw the sound you make? Perhaps at first it will sound like this:

Getting
Started

B,A,G

C&D

F#,E,D

Bb&F

Low C
& C#

High
E-G

G#
& D#

Songbook
ONE

Songbook
TWO

Songbook
THREE

Songbook
FOUR

But after months (or even years!) of practice it should start to sound like:

Tonguing

Most notes on the recorder, to begin with anyway, are started with your tongue pulling back from just behind your upper teeth, as if you were whispering 'Too' or 'Taa'.

When you play several notes one after the other you will usually keep blowing and 'Too, too' the notes rather than doing a separate blow for each one. It should sound something like this looks:

Getting
Started

B,A,G

C&D

F#,E,D

Bb&F

Low C
& C#

High
E-G

G#
& D#

Songbook
ONE

Songbook
TWO

Songbook
THREE

Songbook
FOUR

How Should I Care For My Recorder?

All beginner recorders are plastic so we will concentrate on these. Your recorder should be treated with respect and not left lying around.

Look After It

Take great care of the joints and the fipple because if these are damaged, your recorder will not play well, if at all. Best of all is to dry it

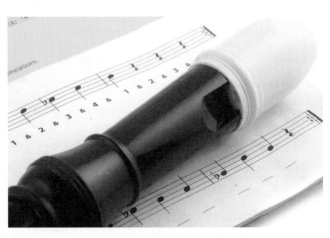

Getting
Started

B,A,G

C&D

F#,E,D

Bb&F

Low C
& C#

High
E-G

G#
& D#

Songbook
ONE

Songbook
TWO

Songbook
THREE

Songbook
FOUR

and put it away in its case as soon as you have
finished playing and put it in a safe place.

No Food Allowed

Keep the inside of your recorder clean,
especially the windway, so do not play it after
eating or drinking (anything but water) without
first brushing your teeth. It is very easy for
small bits of food or dribbles of drink to get
inside the recorder where they make it smelly.

Getting
Started

B,A,G

C♦D

F#,E,D

Bb♦F

Low C
♦ C#

High
E-G

G#
♦ D#

Songbook
ONE

Songbook
TWO

Songbook
THREE

Songbook
FOUR

Drying Out

Shake out any drops of water that might have collected whilst you were blowing.

You can also swab out the inside of the tube with a thin cloth on a stick or a cleaning rod (see picture on the left), if this was supplied with the instrument.

Never force anything else up like a large handkerchief as it could get stuck.

Give It A Wash

Keep your recorder clean by rinsing it through with hand-warm (not hot!) soapy water, followed by cool fresh water (unless you like the taste of soap).

If your recorder has been left with any food particles in it for some time it may smell rather unpleasant, so you may want to also rinse it out with a mild disinfectant or a bicarbonate of soda solution before the fresh water rinse.

Getting Started

B,A,G

C&D

F#,E,D

Bb&F

Low C & C#

High E–G

G# & D#

Songbook ONE

Songbook TWO

Songbook THREE

Songbook FOUR

Getting
Started

B,A,G

C&D

F#,E,D

Bb&F

Low C
& C#

High
E-G

G#
& D#

Songbook
ONE

Songbook
TWO

Songbook
THREE

Songbook
FOUR

Playing The Recorder

Fingering Chart

On the opposite page is the diagram of your recorder that we're going to use in this book.

- Open holes are shown as circles. Holes covered by fingers are dark blobs.

- The six in-line holes are the ones down the front of the instrument and the seventh off-centre hole is the one on the foot joint.

- The blob to the left shows the left thumb hole on the back of the instrument. In this chart this hole is closed and the one opposite it is also closed with your left index finger.

- All of the other holes are open.

- Your recorder will probably have two little holes next to each other for the lowest two simple holes we have shown here. These will be explained when you need to use them.

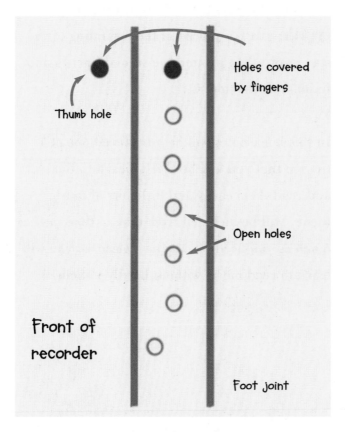

Thumb hole

Holes covered by fingers

Open holes

Front of recorder

Foot joint

Getting
Started

B,A,G

C&D

F#,E,D

Bb&F

Low C
& C#

High
E-G

G#
& D#

Songbook
ONE

Songbook
TWO

Songbook
THREE

Songbook
FOUR

How Is Recorder Music

Written Down?

Music for recorder is written down on a five-line stave (or staff). For descant recorder a **treble clef** is placed at the beginning of the stave, spiralling around the second line up and fixing it as the note G.

In this book notes will be introduced one at a time so that you will be able to learn to finger and read them easily and little bits of music theory will be included from time to time, just as much as you need for any new piece, so you will learn to read music without hardly noticing it.

Getting
Started

B,A,G

C&D

F#,E,D

Bb&F

Low C
& C#

High
E-G

G#
& D#

Songbook
ONE

Songbook
TWO

Songbook
THREE

Songbook
FOUR

Treble or G Clef

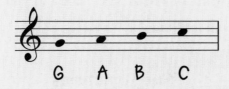

G   A   B   C

The first note is G
The note in the space above G is A
The note on the next line up is B
The note in the next space up is C, and so on

Getting
Started

B,A,G

C&D

F#,E,D

Bb&F

Low C
& C#

High
E–G

G#
& D#

Songbook
ONE

Songbook
TWO

Songbook
THREE

Songbook
FOUR

Counting In Music

To play correct musical **rhythms** you will need to feel how they fit against a **beat**. To begin with you will need to count the beats but after a while this becomes easier and you will forget you are doing it.

Time Signatures

All of the first pieces count the beats in groups of four:

1 2 3 4, 1 2 3 4 and so on.

This is shown by the 'four four' **time signature** at the beginning of each piece, telling you four beats in each group, or **bar**. On the stave, you will see vertical **bar lines** dividing one bar from the next but don't wait at the bar lines, count on from the 4 to the next 1.

The Simple 'Four Four' Beat

To help you count the beat, use anything that makes a simple sound. Examples here show tambourines, castanets and hand claps.

Make sure you count in regular beats:

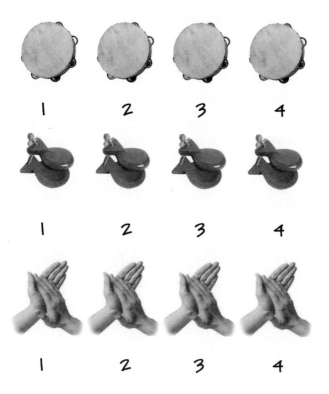

1   2   3   4

1   2   3   4

1   2   3   4

Getting
Started

B,A,G

C&D

F#,E,D

Bb&F

Low C
& C#

High
E–G

G#
& D#

Songbook
ONE

Songbook
TWO

Songbook
THREE

Songbook
FOUR

Getting
Started

B,A,G

C&D

F#,E,D

Bb&F

Low C
& C#

High
E-G

G#
& D#

Songbook
ONE

Songbook
TWO

Songbook
THREE

Songbook
FOUR

Crotchets

In the pieces on the next few pages, each beat that you play is written as a **crochet** (or **quarter note**). Sometimes you will need to take a breath and silent gaps in the music, called **rests**, are still counted just as carefully as the notes you play.

To help you in the first few pieces the count is written in underneath the first bar but you will have to work out for yourself how to count the other bars. Be sure to count the rests (numbers with brackets, like this: (4)) just as evenly as played notes.

Before you start to play each piece, it may help you to count the rhythm out loud, but you can whisper the rests.

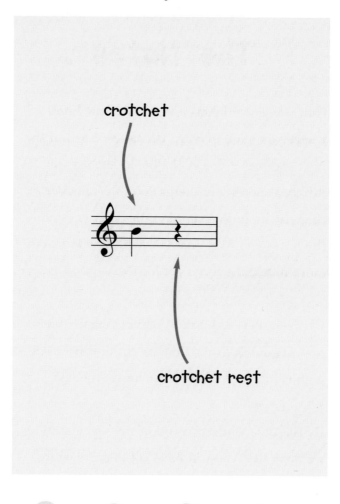

crotchet

crotchet rest

Getting Started

B,A,G

C&D

F#,E,D

Bb&F

Low C & C#

High E-G

G# & D#

Songbook ONE

Songbook TWO

Songbook THREE

Songbook FOUR

Getting
Started

B,A,G

C&D

F#,E,D

Bb&F

Low C
& C#

High
E-G

G#
& D#

Songbook
ONE

Songbook
TWO

Songbook
THREE

Songbook
FOUR

The Notes

Now we get to the exciting part of the book
where you start to learn the notes. Each of the
next seven sections of the book teaches you
different notes, and helps you to remember
them by including simple tunes that contain
the notes you have just learned. As you learn
more notes, the tunes get longer.

Because there is more to playing music than
just the notes, every time we think it is
important, we include some music theory.

By the time you get to end of the seven sections,
we hope that you will have got to grips with
playing the recorder, and will enjoy playing the
tunes that we have chosen for the Songbook.

The Notes

Getting Started

B,A,G

C&D

F#,E,D

Bb&F

Low C & C#

High E-G

G# & D#

Songbook ONE

Songbook TWO

Songbook THREE

Songbook FOUR

New Notes: B, A & G

The Note B

The first note you will need to learn is B. It is written on the middle line of the stave and fingered with your left thumb and first finger.

The note can be any shape but if it is on the middle line it is a B.

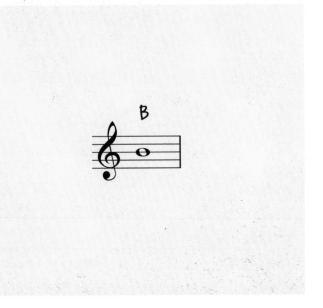

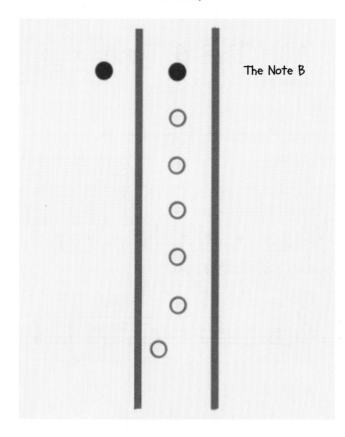

The Note B

Getting
Started

B,A,G

C&D

F#,E,D

Bb&F

Low C
& C#

High
E–G

G#
& D#

Songbook
ONE

Songbook
TWO

Songbook
THREE

Songbook
FOUR

Reminders

It's a good idea to check out the rhythm of a
piece by counting it through before you start to
play. Also count a bar's worth of time in your
head before you begin.

The B Tune

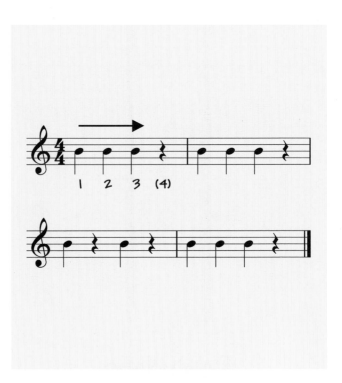

Hints

- Notice which bars are the same (quite a lot of them!)

- Count though before you start. Remember to count the rests (silences) just as rhythmically as the notes and don't slow down for the bar lines.

- Blow the first three notes as if they were one long note (this is what the arrow in the first bar is supposed to remind you to do) but break up that one long note by going 'Too, too, too' with your tongue.

Quick Check

The fingering for B is? (have you learned it yet?)

Getting Started

B,A,G

C&D

F#,E,D

Bb&F

Low C & C#

High E-G

G# & D#

Songbook ONE

Songbook TWO

Songbook THREE

Songbook FOUR

Getting
Started

B,A,G

C&D

F#,E,D

Bb&F

Low C
& C#

High
E-G

G#
& D#

Songbook
ONE

Songbook
TWO

Songbook
THREE

Songbook
FOUR

The Note A

The next tune needs the note A, which is fingered like the B but with your second finger pressed down as well. As you add more fingers, it may be hard at first to keep all of the holes covered. You will get better at this the more you practice.

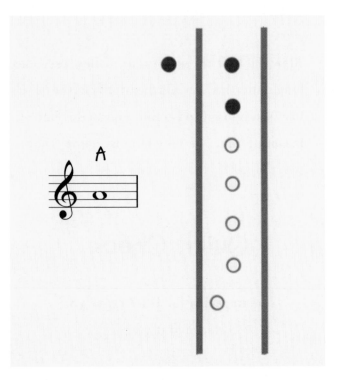

Take The A Tune

• Again, notice which bars are the same and which are different.

• Make sure you don't lose any time going from the first line to the second – read a note or two ahead of your playing if possible and don't hesitate at barlines.

Getting Started

B,A,G

C♭D

F#,E,D

Bb♭F

Low C ♭ C#

High E–G

G# ♭ D#

Songbook ONE

Songbook TWO

Songbook THREE

Songbook FOUR

Getting
Started

B,A,G

C&D

F#,E,D

Bb&F

Low C
& C#

High
E-G

G#
& D#

Songbook
ONE

Songbook
TWO

Songbook
THREE

Songbook
FOUR

The Note G

Now add the third finger of your left hand to make the note G. The more holes your fingers are covering, the more likely you are to have leaks where the finger is not quite over the hole. This happens quite a bit until your fingers learn exactly where to go.

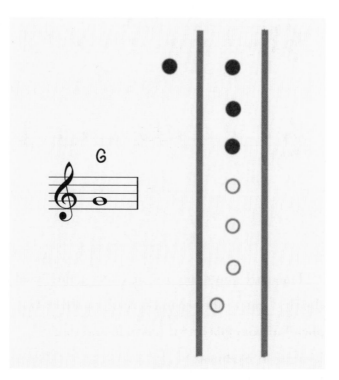

Air On The G Fingering

• This tune is a little bit trickier because of the timing of some of the notes, so count carefully, especially the second line.

Getting Started

B,A,G

C & D

F#,E,D

Bb & F

Low C & C#

High E-G

G# & D#

Songbook ONE

Songbook TWO

Songbook THREE

Songbook FOUR

• Your right fingers shouldn't be touching the recorder except for the thumb, which will be supporting underneath the instrument.

How Am I Doing?

Learning a new skill takes time and patience (and practice!) and to begin with you probably have to think quite hard to remember everything you need to know.

After a while, though, things get a bit easier and you find that you don't have to think about the new things (such as the fingering for a certain note) as much if at all.

But to get to this place you do need to practice, so on the next page are a few tunes that use the notes you've already learned, B, A and G, but mixed together. It would be good to stick with these tunes until you can play them without too much effort before learning the next thing!

Three Tunes on B, A & G

Getting Started

B,A,G

C&D

F#,E,D

Bb&F

Low C & C#

High E–G

G# & D#

Songbook ONE

Songbook TWO

Songbook THREE

Songbook FOUR

• No counts written in here – can you still count the rhythm through before you start to play? Remember to whisper the rests but count them just as rhythmically as the notes.

• There's something slightly different about the third tune – it's five bars long and all of the others have been four bars. Did you spot it?

A & B Together

Getting Started

B,A,G

C&D

F#,E,D

Bb&F

Low C & C#

High E-G

G# & D#

Songbook ONE

Songbook TWO

Songbook THREE

Songbook FOUR

G & A Together

G, A & B Together

A New Rhythm

All of the notes and rests you have seen so far have been exactly one beat long, but how do you write notes that go on longer than one beat?

Minims

The **minim** (also called **half note**) and the **minim rest** last for two crotchets.

Getting Started

B,A,G

C&D

F#,E,D

Bb&F

Low C & C#

High E-G

G# & D#

Songbook ONE

Songbook TWO

Songbook THREE

Songbook FOUR

Getting
Started

B,A,G

C&D

F#,E,D

Bb&F

Low C
& C#

High
E-G

G#
& D#

Songbook
ONE

Songbook
TWO

Songbook
THREE

Songbook
FOUR

You still count two beats but let the note go on for the whole time without tonguing (you 'Too' at the beginning of the note but not on the next beat).

So before we introduce any new notes, on the next page are a few tunes with crotchets and minims mixed up so you will have to count carefully to begin with.

Feeling The Rhythm

Musicians often talk about 'feeling' a rhythm, which means reading and playing it without having to think about it too much. If you play these tunes often enough you will be able to feel the rhythms without having to count them.

Three Tunes With Minims

Aardvark

As there are some new rhythms here, the counting has been written in for you at the beginning.

• The line between the 1 and the 2 is to remind you to keep blowing and not to tongue on the second beat even though you should count it.

Getting Started

B,A,G

C & D

F#,E,D

Bb & F

Low C & C#

High E-G

G# & D#

Songbook ONE

Songbook TWO

Songbook THREE

Songbook FOUR

Bear

• Have you noticed? The tunes are getting a
bit longer.

Caterpillar

• In two places the minim is put right in the
middle of the bar, starting on the second beat.
This is quite alright but you may have to count
the rhythm carefully at first until you get used
to it.

• There are no rests until the last bar so you may need to breathe before you get there. Ticks are often used to show you where to breathe when there are no rests (commas are also used sometimes).

• Whatever you do, don't delay the beat, so make the note before the breath mark just a bit shorter so that you can snatch a breath and come in on time with the next note.

Getting Started

B,A,G

C & D

F#,E,D

Bb & F

Low C & C#

High E-G

G# & D#

Songbook ONE

Songbook TWO

Songbook THREE

Songbook FOUR

New Notes: C & D

Most tunes need a lot more than three notes, so here are two more.

The Note C

C is very similar to B, just with your middle finger rather than the first one.

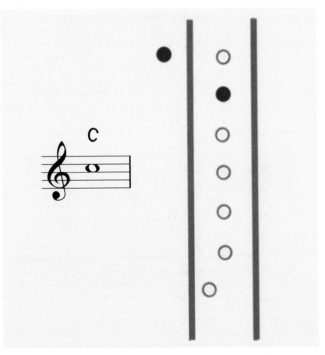

Getting Started

B,A,G

C&D

F#,E,D

Bb&F

Low C & C#

High E-G

G# & D#

Songbook ONE

Songbook TWO

Songbook THREE

Songbook FOUR

The Note D

D may feel a little wobbly at first as you only have one finger on top of the recorder to steady it.

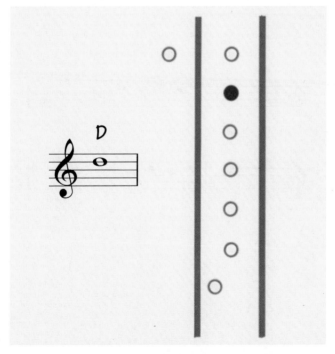

Getting
Started

B,A,G

C&D

F#,E,D

Bb&F

Low C
& C#

High
E–G

G#
& D#

Songbook
ONE

Songbook
TWO

Songbook
THREE

Songbook
FOUR

Two Tunes on C & D

Dolphin

• When you play this tune, can you see a pattern? Tunes are often full of patterns where notes are repeated but usually with a difference.

Elephant

• The next tune has some new rhythms because there are only three beats in each bar (the three four time signature tells you that) so...

...count 1 2 3, 1 2 3

Getting Started

B,A,G

C&D

F#,E,D

Bb&F

Low C & C#

High E–G

G# & D#

Songbook ONE

Songbook TWO

Songbook THREE

Songbook FOUR

Getting
Started

B,A,G

C&D

F#,E,D

Bb&F

Low C
& C#

High
E-G

G#
& D#

Songbook
ONE

Songbook
TWO

Songbook
THREE

Songbook
FOUR

More About Time Signatures

In a simple time signature the upper number tells you how many beats to count and the lower one tells you what kind of note is used to show the beat.

- Crotchets are also known as **quarter notes** so **Four Four** tells you **four** crotchet **beats** to the bar.

- **Three Four** tells you **three** crotchets.
- You can also have **Two Four** and even **Five Four**, though this is much less common.

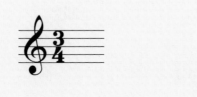

Have you noticed that the time signature comes at the beginning of the first line only?

Getting Started

B,A,G

C♦D

F#,E,D

Bb♦F

Low C ♦ C#

High E-G

G# ♦ D#

Songbook ONE

Songbook TWO

Songbook THREE

Songbook FOUR

Getting
Started

B,A,G

C&D

F#,E,D

Bb&F

Low C
& C#

High
E–G

G#
& D#

Songbook
ONE

Songbook
TWO

Songbook
THREE

Songbook
FOUR

First Tunes

Now that you know five notes, here are some
longer tunes for you to play.

Hills

Waves

Getting
Started

B,A,G

C&D

F#,E,D

Bb&F

Low C
& C#

High
E-G

G#
& D#

Songbook
ONE

Songbook
TWO

Songbook
THREE

Songbook
FOUR

Getting Started

B,A,G

C&D

F#,E,D

Bb&F

Low C & C#

High E–G

G# & D#

Songbook ONE

Songbook TWO

Songbook THREE

Songbook FOUR

Forest

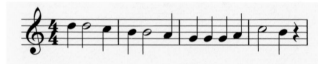

Meadow

• When you add a dot after a minim it lasts for three beats, not two. When you link two notes on the same line or space with a line you must run the notes together as if they were one long note, so the last note in this piece lasts for a whole six beats.

Getting Started

B,A,G

C&D

F#,E,D

Bb&F

Low C & C#

High E–G

G# & D#

Songbook ONE

Songbook TWO

Songbook THREE

Songbook FOUR

Getting
Started

B,A,G

C+D

F#,E,D

Bb&F

Low C
& C#

High
E-G

G#
& D#

Songbook
ONE

Songbook
TWO

Songbook
THREE

Songbook
FOUR

Even More On Rhythm

Before you read the next two tunes we need to look at a few more rhythms.

Semibreves

A note that takes up a whole bar in four four time is called a **semibreve** (or **whole note**) and is written like a minim without the stem:

Quavers

Often a tune will need to have notes that are shorter than a beat. A **quaver** (**eighth note**) is exactly half of a crotchet.

They look similar to crotchets but either have a **flag** when they are separate or are joined by a **beam** when they come in groups.

When you count a rhythm that has quavers, still count the main beats but add the word 'and' (&) between the beats to get the feel of the rhythm.

Getting Started

B,A,G

C&D

F#,E,D

Bb&F

Low C & C#

High E-G

G# & D#

Songbook ONE

Songbook TWO

Songbook THREE

Songbook FOUR

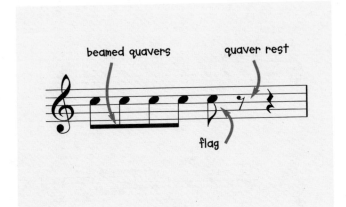

Getting Started

B,A,G

C&D

F#,E,D

Bb&F

Low C & C#

High E-G

G# & D#

Songbook ONE

Songbook TWO

Songbook THREE

Songbook FOUR

Tunes With Quavers & Semibreves

March

Getting
Started

B,A,G

C♦D

F#,E,D

Bb♦F

Low C
♦ C#

High
E–G

G#
♦ D#

Songbook
ONE

Songbook
TWO

Songbook
THREE

Songbook
FOUR

• Often a tune will have some words at the
beginning telling you how to play it. See how
to count quavers.

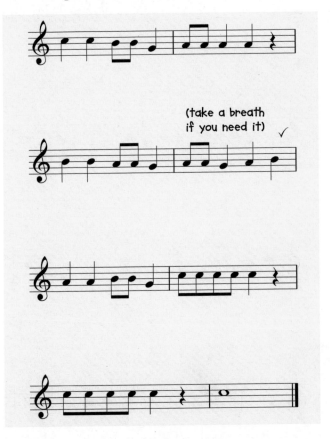

(take a breath
if you need it) ✓

Waltz

• This is our longest tune yet and is divided into sections by double barlines.

• You can make it even longer if you like. When you reach the end, go back to where it says 'Faster' and play the first section of the tune again (up to the double bar in the middle).

Getting
Started

B,A,G

C&D

F#,E,D

Bb&F

Low C
& C#

High
E-G

G#
& D#

Songbook
ONE

Songbook
TWO

Songbook
THREE

Songbook
FOUR

Sad Song

• Sometimes slow tunes can be as hard to play as fast ones because you must blow the notes for a long time. It would be alright to breathe after the semibreves and then after the minims if you have to.

• You can write your own breath marks in. The first section of this tune is repeated as the two dots and the thin/thick barlines tell you to go back to the beginning.

The Notes

Getting Started

B,A,G

C&D

F#,E,D

Bb&F

Low C & C#

High E–G

G# & D#

Songbook ONE

Songbook TWO

Songbook THREE

Songbook FOUR

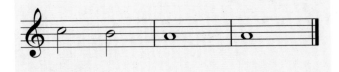

Getting
Started

B,A,G

C&D

F#,E,D

Bb&F

Low C
& C#

High
E-G

G#
& D#

Songbook
ONE

Songbook
TWO

Songbook
THREE

Songbook
FOUR

Scherzo

• The name 'Scherzo' is usually given to pieces that are fast and playful. Be sure to tongue the repeated notes very nimbly. The curved sign over the last note is a **pause**, which means hold the note for a long time (you don't have to count).

Getting Started

B,A,G

C&D

F#,E,D

Bb&F

Low C & C#

High E-G

G# & D#

Songbook ONE

Songbook TWO

Songbook THREE

Songbook FOUR

Ragtime

• The dots above or below a note tell you to play the note **staccato**, a little shorter, but make sure the next note doesn't come in early. Think 'Tat' instead of 'Taa'.

Getting Started

B,A,G

C♦D

F#,E,D

Bb♦F

Low C ♦ C#

High E-G

G# ♦ D#

Songbook ONE

Songbook TWO

Songbook THREE

Songbook FOUR

Getting
Started

B,A,G

C&D

F#,E,D

Bb&F

Low C
& C#

High
E-G

G#
& D#

Songbook
ONE

Songbook
TWO

Songbook
THREE

Songbook
FOUR

• Take care with the third line: some notes are tongued but some must be tied over if you want to get the ragtime effect.

Getting
Started

B,A,G

C&D

F#,E,D

Bb&F

Low C
& C#

High
E-G

G#
& D#

Songbook
ONE

Songbook
TWO

Songbook
THREE

Songbook
FOUR

Just One More Bit Of Rhythm

Look at these two rhythms, almost the same but two notes are tied in the second.

The note that starts on the third beat carries on to half way through the fourth beat.

Getting
Started

B,A,G

C♦D

F#,E,D

Bb♦F

Low C
♦ C#

High
E–G

G#
♦ D#

Songbook
ONE

Songbook
TWO

Songbook
THREE

Songbook
FOUR

There is another way of writing this rhythm
that is often used because the same kind of dot
(after the note) that turns a minim into a three-
beat note can be used to make a crotchet into a
one-and-a-half-beat note. The two halves of the
rhythm below sound the same:

The dot adds half of the length of the note to the
note, so a two-beat note become a three-beat note.
A one-beat note becomes a beat-and-a-half note.

Playthrough One

Now we are equipped to start to play some tunes that were not specially written for this book but are traditional.

When The Saints Go Marching In

• This tune, often called just 'The Saints', was a Gospel song but became one of the most famous Dixieland Jazz tunes of all time.

Getting
Started

B,A,G

C&D

F#,E,D

Bb&F

Low C
& C#

High
E–G

G#
& D#

Songbook
ONE

Songbook
TWO

Songbook
THREE

Songbook
FOUR

• It should be played quite quickly when you have learned the notes, but don't forget the rests.

Merrily We Roll Along

• We've only just learned about dotted crotchets so count this through very carefully! There are no rests in this tune so you will need to plan where to breathe.

Getting Started

B,A,G

C&D

F#,E,D

Bb&F

Low C & C#

High E-G

G# & D#

Songbook ONE

Songbook TWO

Songbook THREE

Songbook FOUR

Dvorak's Largo

• This is the first part of a tune from one of Dvorak's symphonies. Can you play four bars in one breath? If not (yet) then breathe every two bars.

Getting Started

B,A,G

C&D

F#,E,D

Bb&F

Low C & C#

High E–G

G# & D#

Songbook ONE

Songbook TWO

Songbook THREE

Songbook FOUR

New Notes: F#, E & D

It's high time you learned some low notes!

The Note F#

Here is the next note below G, called F#
(F sharp).

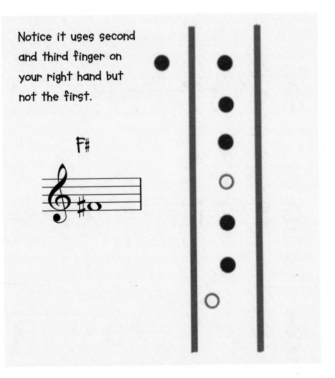

Notice it uses second
and third finger on
your right hand but
not the first.

F#

The Note E

Below F# is E. The fingering is similar to F# so don't mix them up.

Getting Started

B,A,G

C & D

F#,E,D

Bb & F

Low C & C#

High E-G

G# & D#

Songbook ONE

Songbook TWO

Songbook THREE

Songbook FOUR

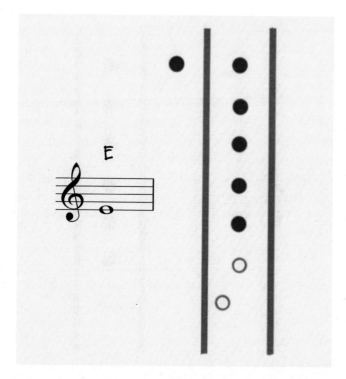

Getting
Started

B,A,G

C&D

F#,E,D

Bb&F

Low C
& C#

High
E-G

G#
& D#

Songbook
ONE

Songbook
TWO

Songbook
THREE

Songbook
FOUR

The Note D

Right down at the bottom is low D. Make sure you cover both little holes.

The more fingers you use, the harder the note becomes to play.

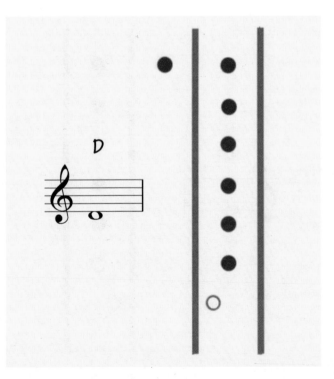

Getting
Started

B,A,G

C&D

F#,E,D

Bb&F

Low C
& C#

High
E–G

G#
& D#

Songbook
ONE

Songbook
TWO

Songbook
THREE

Songbook
FOUR

Playing Low Notes

It's very easy to let some air leak out from under your fingers until you've done lots of practice, so these low notes that use six and seven fingers are harder than the first few you learned. We've given you some very easy exercises to start learning them, one by one.

What is F# (Sharp)?

There is an ordinary F, called F natural, but it's harder to finger than F# (which is a bit higher than F natural) so we'll leave it until later.

Tunes Using Lower Notes

Fox

• The two notes marked * are F♯ as well because they're in the same bar.

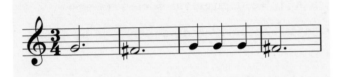

Giraffe

• This tune has only two beats in the bar as the time signature suggests. As in the F♯ tune make sure your two extra E fingers go down together.

Getting Started

B,A,G

C&D

F#,E,D

Bb&F

Low C & C#

High E-G

G# & D#

Songbook ONE

Songbook TWO

Songbook THREE

Songbook FOUR

Hippo

• This tune has both E and F♯ but they don't come together until bar six. Remember your middle finger doesn't move but you swap first and third (like a see-saw).

Iguana

• This has F♯ and E together too. Have you practised swapping your first and third fingers?

Getting Started

B,A,G

C&D

F♯,E,D

Bb&F

Low C & C♯

High E–G

G♯ & D♯

Songbook ONE

Songbook TWO

Songbook THREE

Songbook FOUR

Jellyfish

• Introducing low D, this tune will really test if you are covering all of the holes properly.

Getting Started

B,A,G

C&D

F#,E,D

Bb&F

Low C & C#

High E-G

G# & D#

Songbook ONE

Songbook TWO

Songbook THREE

Songbook FOUR

Kangaroo

• In bars two, four and eight, remember that the second Fs are F♯s too. Do you remember what the circular sign in the last bar means?

Getting Started

B,A,G

C&D

F#,E,D

Bb&F

Low C & C#

High E–G

G# & D#

Songbook ONE

Songbook TWO

Songbook THREE

Songbook FOUR

Playthrough Two

Au Clair De La Lune

• Do you remember what the two dots and double barline mean at the end of bar four? Remind yourself with 'Sad Song' on page 70.

The Notes

The Galway Piper

• Learn this slowly but try playing it faster once you have learned the notes.

• Dots above or below a note mean to shorten it a little but the line above the note in bar six reminds you to play it firmly and full length.

Getting Started

B,A,G

C&D

F#,E,D

Bb&F

Low C & C#

High E-G

G# & D#

Songbook ONE

Songbook TWO

Songbook THREE

Songbook FOUR

Getting
Started

B,A,G

C&D

F#,E,D

Bb&F

Low C
& C#

High
E–G

G#
& D#

Songbook
ONE

Songbook
TWO

Songbook
THREE

Songbook
FOUR

Hot Cross Buns

• The two trickiest bits in this tune are the jump of an octave from high to low D and the run of quavers in the third bar.

• When you come across difficult phrases it's a good idea to practise them separately before you play the whole tune.

• For example, you could invent an exercise like this for the big jump:

• And practise the run slowly at first:

- Notice that both exercises have a repeat sign.

- Now you are ready to play the whole tune:

Getting Started

B,A,G

C & D

F#,E,D

Bb & F

Low C & C#

High E–G

G# & D#

Songbook ONE

Songbook TWO

Songbook THREE

Songbook FOUR

Beethoven's Ode To Joy

• Look out for the tied note at the end of the third line. You will need to count this carefully.

Getting Started

B,A,G

C&D

F#,E,D

Bb&F

Low C & C#

High E-G

G# & D#

Songbook ONE

Songbook TWO

Songbook THREE

Songbook FOUR

Song Of The Volga Boatmen

• The Volga is a big river in Russia. This is just the first part of the tune and you will find the rest later when you know more notes. You will notice some curved lines, called **slurs**, connecting groups of notes in this tune.

Getting Started

B,A,G

C&D

F#,E,D

Bb&F

Low C & C#

High E–G

G# & D#

Songbook ONE

Songbook TWO

Songbook THREE

Songbook FOUR

Getting
Started

B,A,G

C&D

F#,E,D

Bb&F

Low C
& C#

High
E-G

G#
& D#

Songbook
ONE

Songbook
TWO

Songbook
THREE

Songbook
FOUR

New Notes: B♭ & F

The Note B♭

B♭ (B flat) is the note between B and A.

In many tunes it is used instead of the ordinary B (B natural).

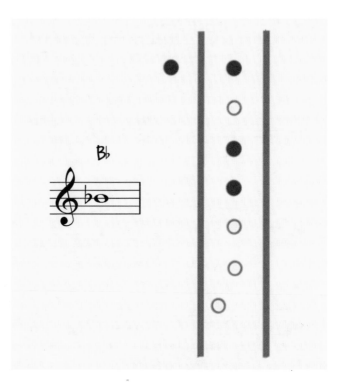

The Note F

Our other new note is F, just below F♯.

Like the B♭, it will help us to play more tunes. Both of these fingerings are more awkward than the earlier ones, but many tunes need them, so on the next few pages are some really simple exercises to help you.

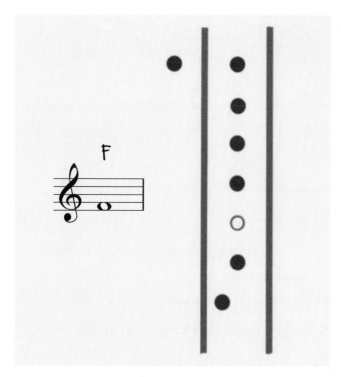

Introducing B♭

The Difference Between B & B♭

• The new sign at the beginning of the second bar is a **natural** , reminding us to play an ordinary B:

• Moving fingers: left hand third and right hand first
• Still fingers: left hand first and thumb
• Notice that some of the notes are slurred

Getting
Started

B,A,G

C&D

F#,E,D

Bb&F

Low C
& C#

High
E-G

G#
& D#

Songbook
ONE

Songbook
TWO

Songbook
THREE

Songbook
FOUR

Connecting Bb With A & G

• Play this as written at first, then try it
slurred. Don't forget to 'Taa' after each breath:

Getting
Started

B,A,G

C&D

F#,E,D

Bb&F

Low C
& C#

High
E-G

G#
& D#

Songbook
ONE

Songbook
TWO

Songbook
THREE

Songbook
FOUR

Connecting B♭ With C

• This is harder slurred than tongued!

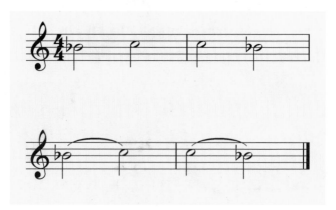

Connecting B♭ With D

• Possibly even harder! Be patient with this:

Tunes With B♭

Crooning Tune

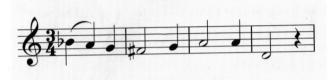

Getting
Started

B,A,G

C&D

F#,E,D

Bb&F

Low C
& C#

High
E-G

G#
& D#

Songbook
ONE

Songbook
TWO

Songbook
THREE

Songbook
FOUR

Introducing F

These easy exercises will help you play the note F. When you can play these little exercises comfortably, you can go on to some tunes that use F (and later both F and B♭).

Ladybird

• To make the F come out clearly in this one, all three fingers on the right hand must be right over the holes.

Getting Started

B,A,G

C&D

F#,E,D

Bb&F

Low C & C#

High E–G

G# & D#

Songbook ONE

Songbook TWO

Songbook THREE

Songbook FOUR

Moose

• The slurred bars will really test if your
fingers are working well.

Getting
Started

B,A,G

C&D

F#,E,D

Bb&F

Low C
& C#

High
E–G

G#
& D#

Songbook
ONE

Songbook
TWO

Songbook
THREE

Songbook
FOUR

Playthrough Three

Merrily We Roll Along (Again!)

• You should have played this tune a few pages back (but starting on B) so it should be quite easy. It's good practice to play the same tune in different keys and we will do this from time to time in this book.

Slow Dance

• Work out where you're going to breathe and put in the ticks (in pencil!). It will sound nice with some of the notes slurred, so add some slurs when you can play it tongued.

Getting Started

B,A,G

C&D

F#,E,D

Bb&F

Low C & C#

High E–G

G# & D#

Songbook ONE

Songbook TWO

Songbook THREE

Songbook FOUR

A-Tisket A-Tasket

• Not all tunes start on the first beat of the bar. This one starts on the fourth, so you might like to count 1 2 3 before coming in with the first note.

• It works really well repeated over and over, so the last bar only has its first three beats, so that you can go right back to the beginning.

The Saints Come Marching Back

• Another version of this tune. It's also a tune that does not start on the first beat, so you would count it in with 1 2 3 4 1 and start playing on the second beat. The last bar has a single beat so that you can repeat it if you want. The really new thing about this version is that it has a **key signature**, which means that every B is played as a B♭ because of the flat at the beginning of each line.

Getting
Started

B,A,G

C&D

F#,E,D

Bb&F

Low C
& C#

High
E-G

G#
& D#

Songbook
ONE

Songbook
TWO

Songbook
THREE

Songbook
FOUR

Key Signatures

When a tune uses a flat or sharp all of the way
through, the signs for these raised or lowered
notes are put at the beginning of each line and
called a key signature. Once you've spotted the
key signature, you're expected to remember to
play all Bs as B♭, for example, or Fs as F♯.

One Flat

The key signature with one flat is either called
the **F major** or **D minor** signature.

One Sharp

The key signature that has one sharp is
G major or **E minor**.

Nothing

No sharps or flats means that the piece is in
C major or **A minor**.

Accidentals

Even with a key signature, some tunes need
notes raising or lowering here and there and
these sharps, flats and naturals are called
accidentals.

There will be more scales later on but that's
enough for now. If you're playing a new piece
and it sounds odd, check if you've missed the
key signature.

Getting Started

B,A,G

C&D

F#,E,D

Bb&F

Low C & C#

High E-G

G# & D#

Songbook ONE

Songbook TWO

Songbook THREE

Songbook FOUR

Getting
Started

B,A,G

C&D

F#,E,D

Bb&F

Low C
& C#

High
E–G

G#
& D#

Songbook
ONE

Songbook
TWO

Songbook
THREE

Songbook
FOUR

First Tunes With Key Signatures

London Bridge Is Falling Down

• Can you play this tune by ear (not looking at the music)? What key is it in?

Twinkle Twinkle

• There is a lot of repetition in this tune; can you say which bars repeat where?

Getting Started

B,A,G

C&D

F#,E,D

Bb&F

Low C & C#

High E-G

G# & D#

Songbook ONE

Songbook TWO

Songbook THREE

Songbook FOUR

Danny Boy

• This tune starts on the second beat. This is just the first half, because the rest of the tune has high notes you don't know yet. It would sound good if you could play each phrase (up to the rest) in one breath, slurred.

Getting
Started

B,A,G

C&D

F#,E,D

Bb&F

Low C
& C#

High
E-G

G#
& D#

Songbook
ONE

Songbook
TWO

Songbook
THREE

Songbook
FOUR

Rocky

• Some of the tied rhythms may seem a little tricky at first. It's alright to leave out the ties at first (if it helps) and put them back in later.

• What does a dot above a note tell you to do?

Getting Started

B,A,G

C&D

F#,E,D

Bb&F

Low C & C#

High E–G

G# & D#

Songbook ONE

Songbook TWO

Songbook THREE

Songbook FOUR

Getting
Started

B,A,G

C&D

F#,E,D

Bb&F

Low C
& C#

High
E-G

G#
& D#

Songbook
ONE

Songbook
TWO

Songbook
THREE

Songbook
FOUR

New Notes: Low C & C#

The Note Low C

Can you play a good low D yet? Because here is an even lower note – and another high one. Low C requires all fingers to seal their holes well so it's not easy.

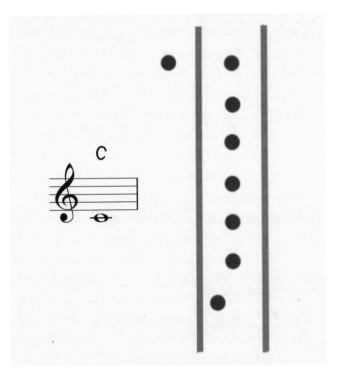

Getting
Started

B,A,G

C&D

F#,E,D

Bb&F

Low C
& C#

High
E-G

G#
& D#

Songbook
ONE

Songbook
TWO

Songbook
THREE

Songbook
FOUR

The Note C#

C# (C sharp) is half way between C and D. It's
fingered like A but with the thumb hole open.

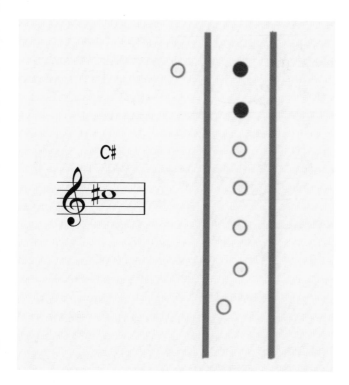

Exercises – Low C & C#

Try playing these exercises that will help you learn the new notes. You can play all of these tongued at first if you like.

Newt

Otter

Peacock

Getting Started

B,A,G

C & D

F#,E,D

Bb & F

Low C & C#

High E-G

G# & D#

Songbook ONE

Songbook TWO

Songbook THREE

Songbook FOUR

Getting
Started

B,A,G

C&D

F#,E,D

Bb&F

Low C
& C#

High
E–G

G#
& D#

Songbook
ONE

Songbook
TWO

Songbook
THREE

Songbook
FOUR

Tunes With Low C

Old Macdonald Had A Farm

• Even though the note B♭ is not used in this tune, there is still a key signature because the tune is in F major.

Johnny Todd

- This is an old English folk song that uses all of the notes of the F scale. There are many different versions of it but they don't usually fit neatly into four four time so there are two bars with two beats here.

- When you know the tune, it's simpler than it looks; just keep counting (or feeling) the crotchet beat.

Getting Started

B,A,G

C&D

F#,E,D

Bb&F

Low C & C#

High E-G

G# & D#

Songbook ONE

Songbook TWO

Songbook THREE

Songbook FOUR

Getting
Started

B,A,G

C&D

F#,E,D

Bb&F

Low C
& C#

High
E-G

G#
& D#

Songbook
ONE

Songbook
TWO

Songbook
THREE

Songbook
FOUR

Tunes With C#

Poor John Patch

• This tune is in D minor which shares a key
signature with F major but it needs a C#
accidental to sound right. It is a **round**, so
several people can play, each one beginning the
tune after waiting a bar.

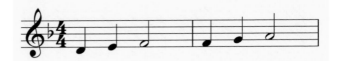

Johnny Has Gone For A Soldier

• An old Irish song sung by a sad girl because her boyfriend has gone to war. There are two sharps in the key signature to remind you to play both F and C as sharps.

Getting Started

B,A,G

C & D

F#,E,D

Bb & F

Low C & C#

High E-G

G# & D#

Songbook ONE

Songbook TWO

Songbook THREE

Songbook FOUR

Hurree Hurroo

• This is an old Scottish love song. Take care: it uses C♯ in the upper register but C natural down at the bottom, which is good because we haven't looked at low C♯ yet.

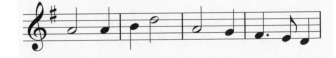

Can Can

• A lively dance tune by the French composer Offenbach. There are two sharps in the key signature again, so remember F♯ and C♯. When you can play it well starting on D, try playing it by ear starting on low C using all natural notes.

Getting Started

B,A,G

C & D

F♯,E,D

B♭ & F

Low C & C♯

High E-G

G♯ & D♯

Songbook ONE

Songbook TWO

Songbook THREE

Songbook FOUR

Getting
Started

B,A,G

C&D

F#,E,D

Bb&F

Low C
& C#

High
E–G

G#
& D#

Songbook
ONE

Songbook
TWO

Songbook
THREE

Songbook
FOUR

Scales

The last tune, the 'Can Can' the, contains a run of all of the notes in the D major scale.

A scale is simply all of the notes in any key played straight up or down and as most music is written in one key or another, musicians often practise scales.

D Major

Here is the D major scale written out as an exercise but you should learn it by heart so that you don't have to look at the notes to play it:

C Major

And here is C major:

We have played some tunes in G and F as well but those scales need some higher notes, so let's get on and learn them.

Getting Started

B,A,G

C&D

F#,E,D

Bb&F

Low C & C#

High E-G

G# & D#

Songbook ONE

Songbook TWO

Songbook THREE

Songbook FOUR

Getting
Started

B,A,G

C & D

F#,E,D

Bb & F

Low C
& C#

High
E–G

G#
& D#

Songbook
ONE

Songbook
TWO

Songbook
THREE

Songbook
FOUR

New Notes: High E &
High F#

The Note High E

High E is fingered like low E but with your
thumbnail in the thumb hole so that it is about
half open and half closed. This is called
pinching or **half-holing** .

The Note High F♯

High F♯ is half holed too. Notice that the right hand is different from the low F♯ fingering.

Getting Started

B,A,G

C♯D

F♯,E,D

B♭♯F

Low C ♯ C♯

High E–G

G♯ ♯ D♯

Songbook ONE

Songbook TWO

Songbook THREE

Songbook FOUR

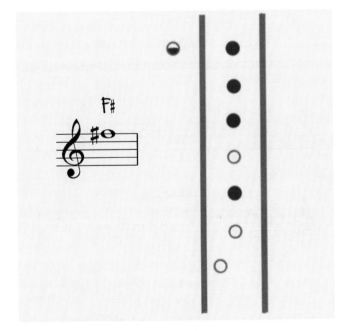

Getting
Started

B,A,G

C&D

F#,E,D

Bb&F

Low C
& C#

High
E–G

G#
& D#

Songbook
ONE

Songbook
TWO

Songbook
THREE

Songbook
FOUR

Introducing High E
& High F♯

• These high notes may be hard to control at first. See which is easier for you; playing them slurred, as written, or with each note tongued. When you can play them confidently go on to some tunes with high notes in them.

Quail

Raccoon

Au Clair De La Lune (In C)

• You may remember playing this a few pages back (page 92). Here it's not only in a new key but the rhythm is written differently too.

• The two-two time signature means two beats to the bar but each beat is a minim (remember a minim is also called a half note). The counting here is exactly the same.

Getting Started

B,A,G

C&D

F#,E,D

Bb&F

Low C & C#

High E–G

G# & D#

Songbook ONE

Songbook TWO

Songbook THREE

Songbook FOUR

131

Getting Started

B,A,G

C&D

F#,E,D

Bb&F

Low C & C#

High E-G

G# & D#

Songbook ONE

Songbook TWO

Songbook THREE

Songbook FOUR

• When you can play the piece as written here, can you play it by ear starting on D? You'll need to use high F♯ and C♯.

Reveille

• You really need a bugle to play this, as it's a wake-up call for soldiers. The crotchets can be played a little **staccato** (short). As the piece starts on the fourth beat, take a breath if you need to before a fourth beat in the fourth bar.

Getting
Started

B,A,G

C&D

F#,E,D

Bb&F

Low C
& C#

High
E-G

G#
& D#

Songbook
ONE

Songbook
TWO

Songbook
THREE

Songbook
FOUR

The Skye Boat Song

• Even though this is a Scottish song, it has some Italian words in it. **D.C.** at the end is short for 'Da Capo' which means 'go back to the beginning' and then you play until the word **Fine**, which means...?

Getting Started

B,A,G

C&D

F#,E,D

Bb&F

Low C & C#

High E-G

G# & D#

Songbook ONE

Songbook TWO

Songbook THREE

Songbook FOUR

Goodnight Irene

• This is a sentimental traditional song and our first high F sharp in a tune.

Getting Started

B,A,G

C&D

F#,E,D

Bb&F

Low C & C#

High E-G

G# & D#

Songbook ONE

Songbook TWO

Songbook THREE

Songbook FOUR

London Bridge Is Falling Down (In A)

• We've seen this tune before in the key of F but here it is a bit higher in the key of A, which has three sharps, though the tune only uses two of them, fortunately the ones you know. The two-two time signature suggests that you feel this rhythm two beats to the bar.

The Minstrel

• You may like to try an alternative fingering for B in this piece, which should make the slurred connections with C smoother (see the next page for this).

Getting Started

B,A,G

C&D

F#,E,D

Bb&F

Low C & C#

High E–G

G# & D#

Songbook ONE

Songbook TWO

Songbook THREE

Songbook FOUR

Getting
Started

B,A,G

C&D

F#,E,D

Bb&F

Low C
& C#

High
E-G

G#
& D#

Songbook
ONE

Songbook
TWO

Songbook
THREE

Songbook
FOUR

Alternative Fingering For The Note B

This B should work on most recorders but still mainly use the one you learned first. It's mostly used to connect smoothly with C.

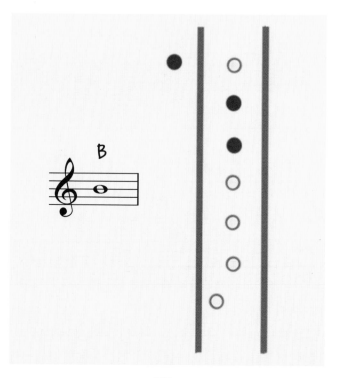

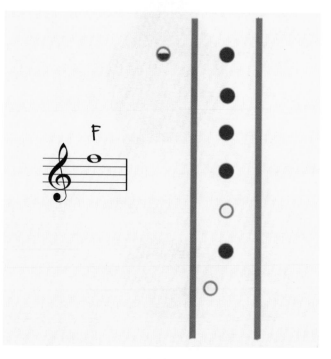

Getting
Started

B,A,G

C&D

F#,E,D

Bb&F

Low C
& C#

High
E-G

G#
& D#

Songbook
ONE

Songbook
TWO

Songbook
THREE

Songbook
FOUR

New Notes: High F & High G

The Note High F

High F is also a pinched note (left thumbnail in the hole) and the right hand fingers are slightly simpler than the lower octave F.

Getting Started

B,A,G

C&D

F#,E,D

Bb&F

Low C & C#

High E-G

G# & D#

Songbook ONE

Songbook TWO

Songbook THREE

Songbook FOUR

The Note High G

High G is fingered exactly like the low one, except for the left thumb.

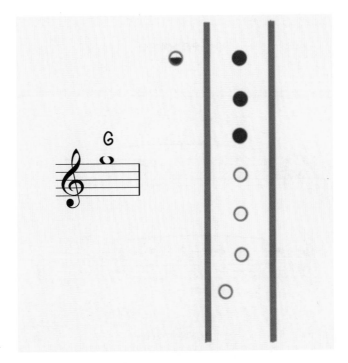

141

Getting
Started

B,A,G

C&D

F#,E,D

Bb&F

Low C
& C#

High
E-G

G#
& D#

Songbook
ONE

Songbook
TWO

Songbook
THREE

Songbook
FOUR

Introducing High F
& High G

These exercises are difficult, especially the end of the second one because of changing from half-holing to normal fingering, so practice it tongued first if you like.

Seahorse

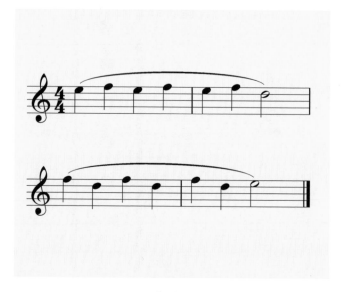

Turtle

Unicorn

Getting Started

B,A,G

C&D

F#,E,D

Bb&F

Low C & C#

High E-G

G# & D#

Songbook ONE

Songbook TWO

Songbook THREE

Songbook FOUR

Connecting High F#
& High G

Vole

• Play these exercises slowly and tongue at first if it helps. It's also good to play tricky bars over and over by themselves.

Woodpecker

Two More Major Scales

Both of these scales should be played tongued and slurred. The top few notes are difficult to connect at first so be patient with yourself as you learn to read and finger them, and play them very slowly at first.

As you practise new tunes or difficult phrases it is fine to play them very slowly at first, but try to keep in strict time, however slow. Don't start too quickly and then have to slow down for the tricky bits.

F Major

G Major

Getting Started

B,A,G

C & D

F#,E,D

Bb & F

Low C & C#

High E-G

G# & D#

Songbook ONE

Songbook TWO

Songbook THREE

Songbook FOUR

Getting
Started

B,A,G

C&D

F#,E,D

Bb&F

Low C
& C#

High
E-G

G#
& D#

Songbook
ONE

Songbook
TWO

Songbook
THREE

Songbook
FOUR

A New Time Signature: Six-Eight

Most of the tunes in the book so far have used quavers to divide the beat into two equal halves, but some tunes need the beat to be divided into threes.

Compound Time

In **compound time** each beat is shown as a dotted crotchet, which of course equals three quavers. The most common form of compound time is **six-eight** with two (not six!) beats to the bar. Here are some common six-eight rhythms.

Tunes With High F & G

• The next two tunes have six quavers in each bar but in six-eight they are felt as two groups of three and in three-four they are three groups of two.

Shanty

Getting Started

B,A,G

C&D

F#,E,D

Bb&F

Low C & C#

High E–G

G# & D#

Songbook ONE

Songbook TWO

Songbook THREE

Songbook FOUR

Carol

Red River Valley

• This is another tune to feel in two, with a minim beat so the last bar is only half length so you can repeat it round if you like. It's fine to count it in four slowly while you're learning it.

Getting
Started

B,A,G

C&D

F#,E,D

Bb&F

Low C
& C#

High
E-G

G#
& D#

Songbook
ONE

Songbook
TWO

Songbook
THREE

Songbook
FOUR

Daisy, Daisy

Getting
Started

B,A,G

C & D

F#,E,D

Bb & F

Low C
& C#

High
E–G

G#
& D#

Songbook
ONE

Songbook
TWO

Songbook
THREE

Songbook
FOUR

Getting
Started

B,A,G

C&D

F#,E,D

Bb&F

Low C
& C#

High
E-G

G#
& D#

Songbook
ONE

Songbook
TWO

Songbook
THREE

Songbook
FOUR

Getting
Started

B,A,G

C & D

F#,E,D

Bb & F

Low C
& C#

High
E-G

G#
& D#

Songbook
ONE

Songbook
TWO

Songbook
THREE

Songbook
FOUR

Tunes With High F# & G

The Daring Young Man On
The Flying Trapeze

• Like the last tune, this is an old music-hall song. It is in the key of D, so remember to play C# as well as the high F#. Breathing in the right

place is important and sometimes there are no rests or breath marks, as in this tune. Often after a long note is a good choice, so where do you plan to breathe in this tune?

The Foggy Foggy Dew

The Notes

Getting
Started

B,A,G

C&D

F#,E,D

Bb&F

Low C
& C#

High
E–G

G#
& D#

Songbook
ONE

Songbook
TWO

Songbook
THREE

Songbook
FOUR

Oh Dear, What Can The Matter Be?

• There is no good place to breathe in the last two lines of this tune, so breathe a little after each dotted crotchet and after the tied not at the end of the second line so that you will have enough breath to last!

• Hopefully the last few tunes have helped you to get to know high F, F# and G, so next we must learn more about rhythm.

Getting
Started

B,A,G

C&D

F#,E,D

Bb&F

Low C
& C#

High
E–G

G#
& D#

Songbook
ONE

Songbook
TWO

Songbook
THREE

Songbook
FOUR

Even Shorter Notes:

Semiquavers

Two quavers fit in the time taken by one crotchet and two **semiquavers** (**sixteenth notes**) fit in the time taken by one quaver, so there are four semiquavers in one crotchet beat. Like

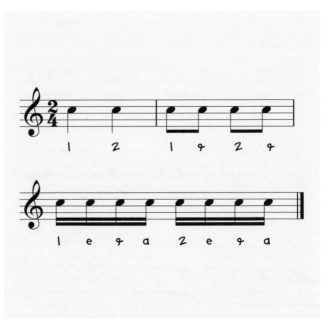

Getting
Started

B,A,G

C&D

F#,E,D

Bb&F

Low C
& C#

High
E-G

G#
& D#

Songbook
ONE

Songbook
TWO

Songbook
THREE

Songbook
FOUR

quavers, semiquavers have flags when they're by themselves and in this example you can see semiquaver rests and some typical rhythms using semiquavers.

Naturals

You will sometimes find the natural sign in music; this cancels sharps or flats in the same bar and can be a reminder if there were an accidental a few bars before.

Pavane

• This is in the style of an old dance. Play it slowly.

• The natural in the third bar is a reminder because you had a sharp in the first bar.

The Notes

Getting Started

B,A,G

C&D

F#,E,D

Bb&F

Low C & C#

High E-G

G# & D#

Songbook ONE

Songbook TWO

Songbook THREE

Songbook FOUR

This Old Man

Dvorak's Largo

• This is the complete version of the tune you learned a part of earlier. Perhaps you can listen to the piece played by an orchestra – it's from Dvorak's 'New World' symphony.

Getting
Started

B,A,G

C & D

F#,E,D

Bb & F

Low C
& C#

High
E-G

G#
& D#

Songbook
ONE

Songbook
TWO

Songbook
THREE

Songbook
FOUR

165

Getting
Started

B,A,G

C&D

F#,E,D

Bb&F

Low C
& C#

High
E-G

G#
& D#

Songbook
ONE

Songbook
TWO

Songbook
THREE

Songbook
FOUR

New Notes: G# & D#

The Note G#

G# is also written as A♭ in flat keys.

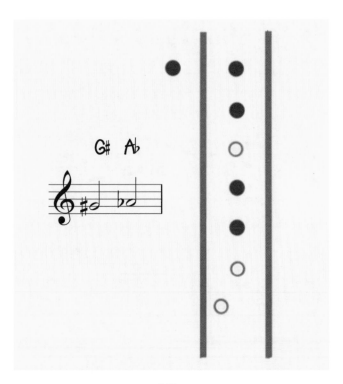

The Note D♯

D♯ is also written as E♭ in flat keys.

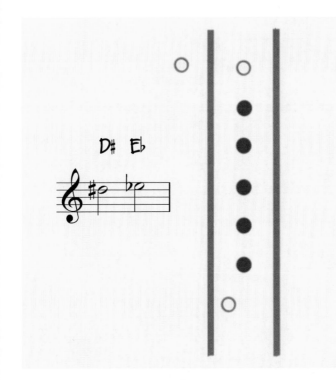

Getting
Started

B,A,G

C♦D

F♯,E,D

Bb♦F

Low C
♦ C♯

High
E-G

G♯
♦ D♯

Songbook
ONE

Songbook
TWO

Songbook
THREE

Songbook
FOUR

Getting
Started

B,A,G

C&D

F#,E,D

Bb&F

Low C
& C#

High
E-G

G#
& D#

Songbook
ONE

Songbook
TWO

Songbook
THREE

Songbook
FOUR

Flats & Sharps

All sharps can also be written as flats. All these have the same fingering:

$$C\sharp = D\flat$$

$$D\sharp = E\flat$$

$$F\sharp = G\flat$$

$$G\sharp = A\flat$$

$$A\sharp = B\flat$$

Getting Started

B,A,G

C&D

F#,E,D

Bb&F

Low C & C#

High E-G

G# & D#

Songbook ONE

Songbook TWO

Songbook THREE

Songbook FOUR

These are all of the notes we are going to use in this book. There are a few more notes on the recorder above high G and there are also low D# and C# fingered by closing only one of the pairs of holes on the lowest notes but we will not need them for the tunes that are to follow.

Know It All

Some fingerings and some keys are easy on the recorder and some are more difficult but to be a good recorder player and play any tune you will need to know them all.

Getting
Started

B,A,G

C&D

F#,E,D

Bb&F

Low C
& C#

High
E-G

G#
& D#

Songbook
ONE

Songbook
TWO

Songbook
THREE

Songbook
FOUR

Some More Scales

A few more major scales using some of the newer notes.

E Major

You don't yet have enough high notes to play some scales right up to the top, so the next two scales double back.

Bb major

A Major

Getting Started

B,A,G

C & D

F#,E,D

Bb & F

Low C & C#

High E-G

G# & D#

Songbook ONE

Songbook TWO

Songbook THREE

Songbook FOUR

Getting
Started

B,A,G

C&D

F#,E,D

Bb&F

Low C
& C#

High
E–G

G#
& D#

Songbook
ONE

Songbook
TWO

Songbook
THREE

Songbook
FOUR

Loud & Soft

Most instruments can play loudly and softly and
part of playing music is carefully following the
volume signs written in the part. This is actually

hardly possible on the recorder because as you blow harder the note gets higher (musicians say 'sharp' meaning out of tune, not the sharp sign you see on the stave). On the other hand, if you blow too gently the note will go 'flat' (again, out of tune).

Dynamics

Much recorder music does not contain 'dynamic' signs to tell you to play louder and softer but you will certainly come across them at some point.

The most usual dynamics are f for 'forte', the Italian for strongly, and p 'piano' softly. Just remember that you will hardly be able to make any difference, compared with other instruments, without going out of tune. If you are playing in a group, perhaps single players can play the soft sections with everyone joining in for the loud bits.

Getting Started

B,A,G

C&D

F#,E,D

Bb&F

Low C & C#

High E-G

G# & D#

Songbook ONE

Songbook TWO

Songbook THREE

Songbook FOUR

Getting
Started

B,A,G

C&D

F#,E,D

Bb&F

Low C
& C#

High
E–G

G#
& D#

Songbook
ONE

Songbook
TWO

Songbook
THREE

Songbook
FOUR

Rhythmic Fun:
Syncopation

Lots of popular music from ragtime on (so that's over 100 years) has used syncopation, which is a way of writing or playing rhythms so that the beat is 'hidden'. You can't really play pop or jazz tunes without syncopating. It has slipped into one or two tunes so far, but let's look at it more closely:

The Offbeat

The count in the first bar can be repeated, but in the second bar the note on '3 &' is carried on and you count '4' without tonguing it. Bar three is the same as bar two, just written more simply, the crotchet starting on '3 &' is called an 'offbeat' note.

Tap Your Feet!

It's always very important when playing syncopated notes such as this one to keep feeling the beat. Many people tap their foot (or toes inside their shoes – it's quieter) to keep the beat, so see if this helps you keep a steady beat whilst playing strong syncopations.

Try These Out

The next few exercises and tunes use syncopations that start easy but gradually get harder until the last few are really tricky. Don't worry if you can't play them all at first but come back to them later when you've done more playing.

Getting Started

B,A,G

C&D

F#,E,D

Bb&F

Low C & C#

High E–G

G# & D#

Songbook ONE

Songbook TWO

Songbook THREE

Songbook FOUR

Getting
Started

B,A,G

C & D

F#,E,D

Bb & F

Low C
& C#

High
E–G

G#
& D#

Songbook
ONE

Songbook
TWO

Songbook
THREE

Songbook
FOUR

Syncopated Playthrough

Xanadu

• In the fourth bar you suddenly have to do the same syncopation again.

Cakewalk

• This is the beginning of a piece by the French composer Debussy inspired by ragtime.

Raggy Doll

• **This exercise looks different because it has rests but the rhythm is really very similar.**

Getting Started

B,A,G

C & D

F#,E,D

Bb & F

Low C & C#

High E–G

G# & D#

Songbook ONE

Songbook TWO

Songbook THREE

Songbook FOUR

Getting
Started

B,A,G

C&D

F#,E,D

Bb&F

Low C
& C#

High
E-G

G#
& D#

Songbook
ONE

Songbook
TWO

Songbook
THREE

Songbook
FOUR

Granite (It's A Rock!)

• Make sure you keep a strong sense of the beat at all times but especially when a tie goes over a bar line.

The Notes

Getting Started

B,A,G

C&D

F#,E,D

Bb&F

Low C & C#

High E-G

G# & D#

Songbook ONE

Songbook TWO

Songbook THREE

Songbook FOUR

Getting
Started

B,A,G

C&D

F#,E,D

Bb&F

Low C
& C#

High
E-G

G#
& D#

Songbook
ONE

Songbook
TWO

Songbook
THREE

Songbook
FOUR

Basalt (Yes, Another Rock)

• Syncopations can occur in three-four as well!
Don't forget to count through the long notes as
carefully as you count the syncopations.

The Notes

Getting
Started

B,A,G

C&D

F#,E,D

Bb&F

Low C
& C#

High
E-G

G#
& D#

Songbook
ONE

Songbook
TWO

Songbook
THREE

Songbook
FOUR

Yucca

• Syncopations can be made with ties, like in the first bar, or by putting a rest after an offbeat note, like in the second. Make sure your last note finishes right on '4 ♪'.

Zig-Zag

• This is similar to the last exercise. Count the rests in full.

Jumping

- More offbeats in a row, so keep the beat.

Bring The Beat Back

- Even more offbeats! When you have an onbeat note after syncopations, be careful that it is played right on the beat.

Getting Started

B,A,G

C&D

F#,E,D

Bb&F

Low C & C#

High E-G

G# & D#

Songbook ONE

Songbook TWO

Songbook THREE

Songbook FOUR

Quartz

• This could be played quite quickly when you have learned the notes and rhythms.

Getting Started

B,A,G

C&D

F#,E,D

Bb&F

Low C & C#

High E-G

G# & D#

Songbook ONE

Songbook TWO

Songbook THREE

Songbook FOUR

• **As ever, make sure the rests are full length.**

Getting
Started

B,A,G

C & D

F#,E,D

Bb & F

Low C
& C#

High
E–G

G#
& D#

Songbook
ONE

Songbook
TWO

Songbook
THREE

Songbook
FOUR

Feldspar

- This tune has semiquavers so don't play it too quickly.

The Notes

Getting
Started

B,A,G

C&D

F#,E,D

Bb&F

Low C
& C#

High
E–G

G#
& D#

Songbook
ONE

Songbook
TWO

Songbook
THREE

Songbook
FOUR

Vega

• Syncopations involving semiquavers are always trickier – this is just a taster.

Sirius

• And here it's the semiquavers themselves that are syncopated. Notice exactly which notes are tied and which are not.

Mimosa

• In the second bar the notes on the first and second beats should sound the same, it's just the writing of the second one is simpler.

Adara

• The first two beats are very like the next two – can you see how they are related?

Getting Started

B,A,G

C&D

F#,E,D

Bb&F

Low C & C#

High E–G

G# & D#

Songbook ONE

Songbook TWO

Songbook THREE

Songbook FOUR

Shale

• Take this very steadily, with all its semiquavers. If the syncopations are too difficult at first, try playing without the ties.

Getting Started

B,A,G

C&D

F#,E,D

Bb&F

Low C & C#

High E–G

G# & D#

Songbook ONE

Songbook TWO

Songbook THREE

Songbook FOUR

Getting Started

B,A,G

C&D

F#,E,D

Bb&F

Low C & C#

High E-G

G# & D#

Songbook ONE

Songbook TWO

Songbook THREE

Songbook FOUR

Conglomerate

• This is really tricky – in fact it's the hardest bit of rhythmic reading in the whole book, so when you can play it accurately you can be really proud of yourself. As with all pieces with semiquavers, learn it at a very slow tempo.

The Notes

Getting
Started

B,A,G

C&D

F#,E,D

Bb&F

Low C
& C#

High
E-G

G#
& D#

Songbook
ONE

Songbook
TWO

Songbook
THREE

Songbook
FOUR

Getting
Started

B,A,G

C&D

F#,E,D

Bb&F

Low C
& C#

High
E-G

G#
& D#

Songbook
ONE

Songbook
TWO

Songbook
THREE

Songbook
FOUR

Minor Scales

There are different kinds of minor scales, so we will look at just a few examples here.

E Natural Minor

The simplest kind of minor scale is simply a major scale but starting on its sixth note. You already know G major (see page 147) so E minor is:

E Harmonic Minor

This version is called Harmonic Minor because it is mostly used to create chords to accompany minor tunes:

Dorian Mode

Another folksy-sounding minor scale is the Dorian Mode. This has a raised sixth note.

E Melodic Minor

Finally, the Melodic Minor scale has both a raised sixth and seventh on the way up but lower versions of these notes on the way down.

You will find a few minor scales in different keys on the next two pages. Musicians often practise scales because so much music is written using scales that if your fingers know the scales already, you can play them much more easily.

D Natural Minor

D Harmonic Minor

D Dorian

D Melodic Minor

G Natural Minor

G Harmonic Minor

G Dorian

G Melodic Minor

Getting Started
B,A,G
C & D
F#,E,D
Bb & F
Low C & C#
High E-G
G# & D#
Songbook ONE
Songbook TWO
Songbook THREE
Songbook FOUR

Getting
Started

B,A,G

C&D

F#,E,D

Bb&F

Low C
& C#

High
E-G

G#
& D#

Songbook
ONE

Songbook
TWO

Songbook
THREE

Songbook
FOUR

Songbook

Now that you've learned the basics, you need lots of practice playing tunes in different styles. So from here on there are very few words but lots of tunes. You can tackle them in any order you like but we've put a selection of the easier ones first to get you started. Each tune has a set of chords above which can be played on guitar or piano – or you can just play the tunes by themselves of course.

Songbook One

Songbook Two

Songbook Three

Songbook Four

Getting Started

B,A,G

C&D

F#,E,D

Bb&F

Low C & C#

High E-G

G# & D#

Songbook ONE

Songbook TWO

Songbook THREE

Songbook FOUR

A Hunting We Will Go

Getting
Started

B,A,G

C&D

F#,E,D

Bb&F

Low C
& C#

High
E-G

G#
& D#

Songbook
ONE

Songbook
TWO

Songbook
THREE

Songbook
FOUR

Gavotte

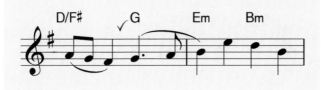

Getting Started

B,A,G

C&D

F#,E,D

Bb&F

Low C & C#

High E-G

G# & D#

Songbook ONE

Songbook TWO

Songbook THREE

Songbook FOUR

Kumbaya

Getting
Started

B,A,G

C&D

F#,E,D

Bb&F

Low C
& C#

High
E-G

G#
& D#

Songbook
ONE

Songbook
TWO

Songbook
THREE

Songbook
FOUR

Shortnin' Bread

Getting
Started

B,A,G

C&D

F#,E,D

Bb&F

Low C
& C#

High
E-G

G#
& D#

Songbook
ONE

Songbook
TWO

Songbook
THREE

Songbook
FOUR

I Saw Three Ships

Getting Started

B,A,G

C&D

F#,E,D

Bb&F

Low C & C#

High E–G

G# & D#

Songbook ONE

Songbook TWO

Songbook THREE

Songbook FOUR

The Knight And The Shepherd's Daughter

Getting Started

B,A,G

C&D

F#,E,D

Bb&F

Low C & C#

High E-G

G# & D#

Songbook ONE

Songbook TWO

Songbook THREE

Songbook FOUR

Lavender's Blue

(D major)

Getting Started

B,A,G

C&D

F#,E,D

Bb&F

Low C & C#

High E-G

G# & D#

Songbook ONE

Songbook TWO

Songbook THREE

Songbook FOUR

Lavender's Blue

(F major)

Getting Started

B,A,G

C & D

F#,E,D

Bb & F

Low C & C#

High E-G

G# & D#

Songbook ONE

Songbook TWO

Songbook THREE

Songbook FOUR

Auld Lang Syne

Getting Started

B, A, G

C & D

F#, E, D

Bb & F

Low C & C#

High E-G

G# & D#

Songbook ONE

Songbook TWO

Songbook THREE

Songbook FOUR

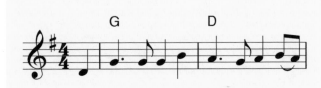

Getting
Started

B,A,G

C&D

F#,E,D

Bb&F

Low C
& C#

High
E-G

G#
& D#

Songbook
ONE

Songbook
TWO

Songbook
THREE

Songbook
FOUR

Morning Has Broken

Getting
Started

B,A,G

C&D

F#,E,D

Bb&F

Low C
& C#

High
E-G

G#
& D#

Songbook
ONE

Songbook
TWO

Songbook
THREE

Songbook
FOUR

Minuet

Getting
Started

B, A, G

C & D

F#, E, D

Bb & F

Low C
& C#

High
E–G

G#
& D#

Songbook
ONE

Songbook
TWO

Songbook
THREE

Songbook
FOUR

Getting Started

B,A,G

C&D

F#,E,D

Bb&F

Low C & C#

High E-G

G# & D#

Songbook ONE

Songbook TWO

Songbook THREE

Songbook FOUR

Scarborough Fair

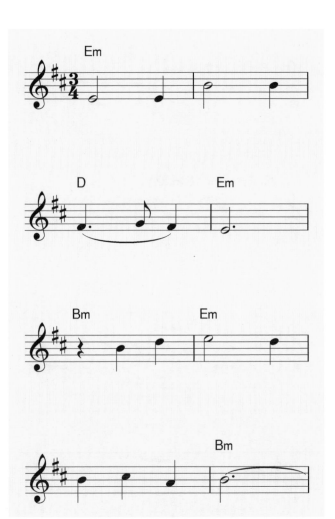

Getting
Started

B,A,G

C&D

F#,E,D

Bb&F

Low C
& C#

High
E-G

G#
& D#

Songbook
ONE

Songbook
TWO

Songbook
THREE

Songbook
FOUR

The Streets of Laredo

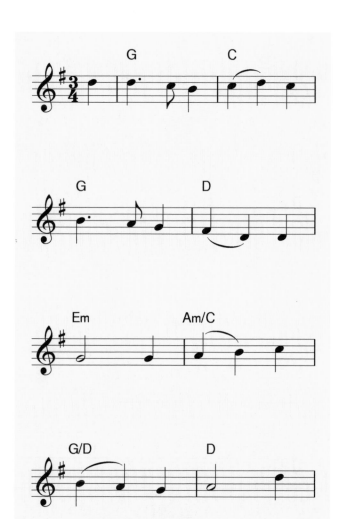

Getting Started

B,A,G

C&D

F#,E,D

Bb&F

Low C & C#

High E-G

G# & D#

Songbook ONE

Songbook TWO

Songbook THREE

Songbook FOUR

My Bonnie Lies Over The Ocean

Getting Started

B,A,G

C&D

F#,E,D

Bb&F

Low C & C#

High E-G

G# & D#

Songbook ONE

Songbook TWO

Songbook THREE

Songbook FOUR

Getting Started

B,A,G

C&D

F#,E,D

Bb&F

Low C & C#

High E-G

G# & D#

Songbook ONE

Songbook TWO

Songbook THREE

Songbook FOUR

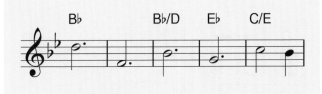

When Johnny Comes Marching Home Again

Getting
Started

B,A,G

C&D

F#,E,D

Bb&F

Low C
& C#

High
E-G

G#
& D#

Songbook
ONE

Songbook
TWO

Songbook
THREE

Songbook
FOUR

Getting Started

B,A,G

C&D

F#,E,D

Bb&F

Low C & C#

High E-G

G# & D#

Songbook ONE

Songbook TWO

Songbook THREE

Songbook FOUR

Getting
Started

B,A,G

C&D

F#,E,D

Bb&F

Low C
& C#

High
E-G

G#
& D#

Songbook
ONE

Songbook
TWO

Songbook
THREE

Songbook
FOUR

Rounds

A round is a tune that can accompany itself if you have two or more players. The first player or group starts and when they get to the arrow, the next one joins in. You can have as many different parts as you like.

Some rounds stop all together on a pause and some you just play for as many times as you want and then just drop out.

Frère Jacques

Getting Started

B,A,G

C&D

F#,E,D

Bb&F

Low C & C#

High E-G

G# & D#

Songbook ONE

Songbook TWO

Songbook THREE

Songbook FOUR

Hey Ho

Poor John Patch

Getting Started

B,A,G

C&D

F#,E,D

Bb&F

Low C & C#

High E–G

G# & D#

Songbook ONE

Songbook TWO

Songbook THREE

Songbook FOUR

Poor John Patch (con't)

This tune can work in several keys. It's good practice to play tunes in different keys, but quite a challenge. Only one key at a time, though!

Kookaburra

Getting Started

B,A,G

C&D

F#,E,D

Bb&F

Low C & C#

High E-G

G# & D#

Songbook ONE

Songbook TWO

Songbook THREE

Songbook FOUR

Shalom Chaverin

Getting
Started

B,A,G

C&D

F#,E,D

Bb&F

Low C
& C#

High
E–G

G#
& D#

Songbook
ONE

Songbook
TWO

Songbook
THREE

Songbook
FOUR

London's Burning

Getting Started

B,A,G

C&D

F#,E,D

Bb&F

Low C & C#

High E-G

G# & D#

Songbook ONE

Songbook TWO

Songbook THREE

Songbook FOUR

Serenity

Getting Started

B,A,G

C & D

F#,E,D

Bb & F

Low C & C#

High E-G

G# & D#

Songbook ONE

Songbook TWO

Songbook THREE

Songbook FOUR

Row Your Boat

Getting Started

B,A,G

C&D

F#,E,D

Bb&F

Low C & C#

High E-G

G# & D#

Songbook ONE

Songbook TWO

Songbook THREE

Songbook FOUR

Getting Started

To Stop The Train

Come in on either arrow.

B,A,G

C&D

F#,E,D

Bb&F

Low C & C#

High E-G

G# & D#

Songbook ONE

Songbook TWO

Songbook THREE

Songbook FOUR

The Tallis Canon

Getting Started

B,A,G

C&D

F#,E,D

Bb&F

Low C & C#

High E-G

G# & D#

Songbook ONE

Songbook TWO

Songbook THREE

Songbook FOUR

233

All Through The Night

Getting
Started

B,A,G

C&D

F#,E,D

Bb&F

Low C
& C#

High
E-G

G#
& D#

Songbook
ONE

Songbook
TWO

Songbook
THREE

Songbook
FOUR

The Ash Grove

Getting Started

B,A,G

C&D

F#,E,D

Bb&F

Low C & C#

High E-G

G# & D#

Songbook ONE

Songbook TWO

Songbook THREE

Songbook FOUR

Getting Started

B,A,G

C & D

F#,E,D

Bb & F

Low C & C#

High E-G

G# & D#

Songbook ONE

Songbook TWO

Songbook THREE

Songbook FOUR

237

The Bamboo Flute

Accompany with fifths; F and C.

Getting Started

B,A,G

C&D

F#,E,D

Bb&F

Low C & C#

High E-G

G# & D#

Songbook ONE

Songbook TWO

Songbook THREE

Songbook FOUR

Getting
Started

B,A,G

C&D

F#,E,D

Bb&F

Low C
& C#

High
E-G

G#
& D#

Songbook
ONE

Songbook
TWO

Songbook
THREE

Songbook
FOUR

The Banana Boat Song

Getting Started

B,A,G

C&D

F#,E,D

Bb&F

Low C & C#

High E-G

G# & D#

Songbook ONE

Songbook TWO

Songbook THREE

Songbook FOUR

Believe Me, If All Those Endearing Young Charms

Getting Started

B,A,G

C&D

F#,E,D

Bb&F

Low C & C#

High E–G

G# & D#

Songbook ONE

Songbook TWO

Songbook THREE

Songbook FOUR

Getting Started

B,A,G

C&D

F#,E,D

Bb&F

Low C & C#

High E–G

G# & D#

Songbook ONE

Songbook TWO

Songbook THREE

Songbook FOUR

The Bear Went Over The Mountain

Getting Started

B,A,G

C&D

F#,E,D

Bb&F

Low C & C#

High E-G

G# & D#

Songbook ONE

Songbook TWO

Songbook THREE

Songbook FOUR

Billy Boy

Getting Started

B,A,G

C&D

F#,E,D

Bb&F

Low C & C#

High E-G

G# & D#

Songbook ONE

Songbook TWO

Songbook THREE

Songbook FOUR

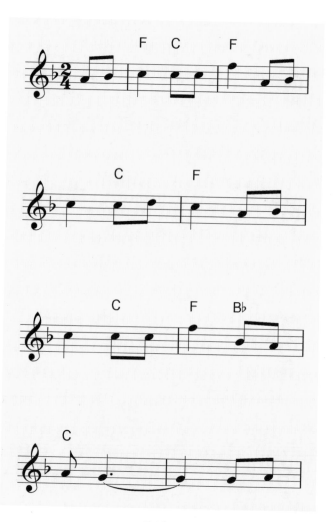

Getting Started

B,A,G

C&D

F#,E,D

Bb&F

Low C & C#

High E-G

G# & D#

Songbook ONE

Songbook TWO

Songbook THREE

Songbook FOUR

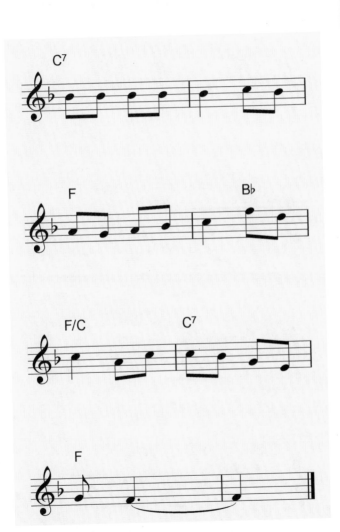

Black Is The Colour of My True Love's Hair

The Blue Tailed Fly

This is also known as 'Jimmy Crack Corn'.

Getting Started

B,A,G

C&D

F#,E,D

Bb&F

Low C & C#

High E-G

G# & D#

Songbook ONE

Songbook TWO

Songbook THREE

Songbook FOUR

The Lincolnshire Poacher

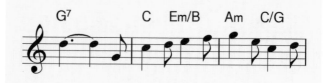

Getting
Started

B,A,G

C&D

F#,E,D

Bb&F

Low C
& C#

High
E-G

G#
& D#

Songbook
ONE

Songbook
TWO

Songbook
THREE

Songbook
FOUR

Oleanna

Getting
Started

B,A,G

C&D

F#,E,D

Bb&F

Low C
& C#

High
E-G

G#
& D#

Songbook
ONE

Songbook
TWO

Songbook
THREE

Songbook
FOUR

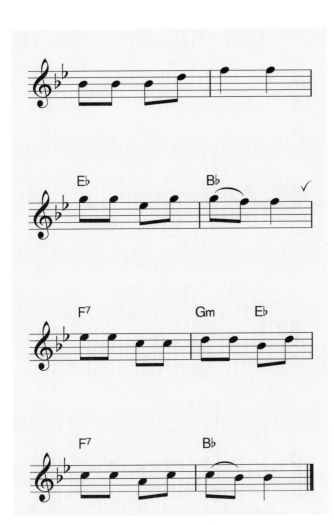

Getting Started

B,A,G

C&D

F#,E,D

Bb&F

Low C & C#

High E-G

G# & D#

Songbook ONE

Songbook TWO

Songbook THREE

Songbook FOUR

Sakura

This is best unaccompanied but your could add
a drone on E if you really want to.

Getting
Started

B,A,G

C&D

F#,E,D

Bb&F

Low C
& C#

High
E-G

G#
& D#

Songbook
ONE

Songbook
TWO

Songbook
THREE

Songbook
FOUR

N.C.*

Getting Started

B,A,G

C&D

F#,E,D

Bb&F

Low C & C#

High E–G

G# & D#

Songbook ONE

Songbook TWO

Songbook THREE

Songbook FOUR

Ach Du Lieber Augustin

Getting
Started

B,A,G

C&D

F#,E,D

Bb&F

Low C
& C#

High
E-G

G#
& D#

Songbook
ONE

Songbook
TWO

Songbook
THREE

Songbook
FOUR

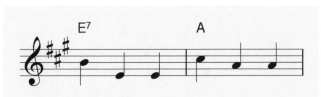

Men Of Harlech

Getting Started

B,A,G

C&D

F#,E,D

Bb&F

Low C & C#

High E-G

G# & D#

Songbook ONE

Songbook TWO

Songbook THREE

Songbook FOUR

Getting
Started

B,A,G

C & D

F#,E,D

Bb & F

Low C
& C#

High
E-G

G#
& D#

Songbook
ONE

Songbook
TWO

Songbook
THREE

Songbook
FOUR

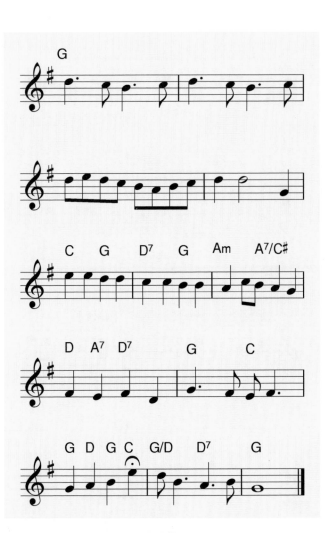

Alouette

Getting Started

B,A,G

C&D

F#,E,D

Bb&F

Low C & C#

High E–G

G# & D#

Songbook ONE

Songbook TWO

Songbook THREE

Songbook FOUR

Songbook Two: Folk & Sea Songs

Getting Started

B,A,G

C & D

F#,E,D

Bb & F

Low C & C#

High E-G

G# & D#

Songbook ONE

Songbook TWO

Songbook THREE

Songbook FOUR

Blow Away The Morning Dew

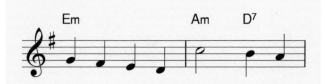

Getting
Started

B,A,G

C&D

F#,E,D

Bb&F

Low C
& C#

High
E-G

G#
& D#

Songbook
ONE

Songbook
TWO

Songbook
THREE

Songbook
FOUR

Linstead Market

Getting Started

B,A,G

C&D

F#,E,D

Bb&F

Low C & C#

High E-G

G# & D#

Songbook ONE

Songbook TWO

Songbook THREE

Songbook FOUR

Getting Started

B,A,G

C&D

F#,E,D

Bb&F

Low C & C#

High E-G

G# & D#

Songbook ONE

Songbook TWO

Songbook THREE

Songbook FOUR

Lil' Liza Jane

Getting
Started

B,A,G

C&D

F#,E,D

Bb&F

Low C
& C#

High
E–G

G#
& D#

Songbook
ONE

Songbook
TWO

Songbook
THREE

Songbook
FOUR

The British Grenadiers

Getting Started

B,A,G

C&D

F#,E,D

Bb&F

Low C & C#

High E-G

G# & D#

Songbook ONE

Songbook TWO

Songbook THREE

Songbook FOUR

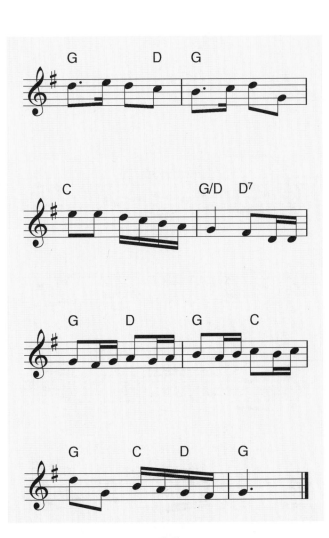

Getting
Started

B,A,G

C&D

F#,E,D

Bb&F

Low C
& C#

High
E-G

G#
& D#

Songbook
ONE

Songbook
TWO

Songbook
THREE

Songbook
FOUR

Canción De Maja

Getting Started

B,A,G

C&D

F#,E,D

Bb&F

Low C & C#

High E-G

G# & D#

Songbook ONE

Songbook TWO

Songbook THREE

Songbook FOUR

Getting Started

B,A,G

C&D

F#,E,D

Bb&F

Low C & C#

High E-G

G# & D#

Songbook ONE

Songbook TWO

Songbook THREE

Songbook FOUR

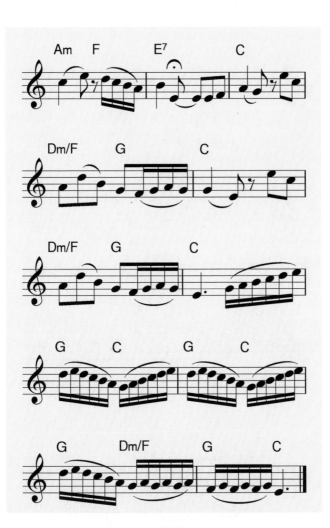

Matilda

Getting Started

B,A,G

C & D

F#,E,D

Bb & F

Low C & C#

High E–G

G# & D#

Songbook ONE

Songbook TWO

Songbook THREE

Songbook FOUR

Santa Lucia

Getting Started

B,A,G

C&D

F#,E,D

Bb&F

Low C & C#

High E-G

G# & D#

Songbook ONE

Songbook TWO

Songbook THREE

Songbook FOUR

Getting
Started

B,A,G

C&D

F#,E,D

Bb&F

Low C
& C#

High
E-G

G#
& D#

Songbook
ONE

Songbook
TWO

Songbook
THREE

Songbook
FOUR

As I Roved Out

Getting Started

B,A,G

C&D

F#,E,D

Bb&F

Low C & C#

High E-G

G# & D#

Songbook ONE

Songbook TWO

Songbook THREE

Songbook FOUR

Brown Girl In The Ring

Getting Started

B,A,G

C&D

F#,E,D

Bb&F

Low C & C#

High E-G

G# & D#

Songbook ONE

Songbook TWO

Songbook THREE

Songbook FOUR

A-Rovin'

Getting Started

B,A,G

C&D

F#,E,D

Bb&F

Low C & C#

High E-G

G# & D#

Songbook ONE

Songbook TWO

Songbook THREE

Songbook FOUR

Getting Started

B,A,G

C&D

F#,E,D

Bb&F

Low C & C#

High E-G

G# & D#

Songbook ONE

Songbook TWO

Songbook THREE

Songbook FOUR

What Shall We Do With A Drunken Sailor

Getting Started

B,A,G

C&D

F#,E,D

Bb&F

Low C & C#

High E-G

G# & D#

Songbook ONE

Songbook TWO

Songbook THREE

Songbook FOUR

Getting
Started

B,A,G

C&D

F#,E,D

Bb&F

Low C
& C#

High
E-G

G#
& D#

Songbook
ONE

Songbook
TWO

Songbook
THREE

Songbook
FOUR

When Johnny Comes Down To Hilo

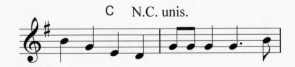

Getting Started

B,A,G

C&D

F#,E,D

Bb&F

Low C & C#

High E-G

G# & D#

Songbook ONE

Songbook TWO

Songbook THREE

Songbook FOUR

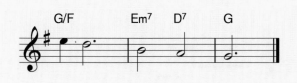

The Rambling Sailor

Getting Started

B,A,G

C♭D

F#,E,D

Bb♭F

Low C ♭ C#

High E-G

G# ♭ D#

Songbook ONE

Songbook TWO

Songbook THREE

Songbook FOUR

Getting Started

B,A,G

C&D

F#,E,D

Bb&F

Low C & C#

High E-G

G# & D#

Songbook ONE

Songbook TWO

Songbook THREE

Songbook FOUR

Blow The Man Down

Getting
Started

B,A,G

C & D

F#,E,D

Bb & F

Low C
& C#

High
E-G

G#
& D#

Songbook
ONE

Songbook
TWO

Songbook
THREE

Songbook
FOUR

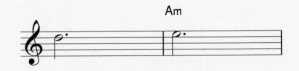

Getting
Started

B,A,G

C&D

F#,E,D

Bb&F

Low C
& C#

High
E-G

G#
& D#

Songbook
ONE

Songbook
TWO

Songbook
THREE

Songbook
FOUR

Bobby Shaftoe

Getting
Started

B,A,G

C&D

F#,E,D

Bb&F

Low C
& C#

High
E-G

G#
& D#

Songbook
ONE

Songbook
TWO

Songbook
THREE

Songbook
FOUR

Getting Started

B,A,G

C&D

F#,E,D

Bb&F

Low C & C#

High E-G

G# & D#

Songbook ONE

Songbook TWO

Songbook THREE

Songbook FOUR

Bound For South Australia

Getting
Started

B,A,G

C&D

F#,E,D

Bb&F

Low C
& C#

High
E-G

G#
& D#

Songbook
ONE

Songbook
TWO

Songbook
THREE

Songbook
FOUR

Getting
Started

B,A,G

C & D

F#,E,D

Bb & F

Low C
& C#

High
E–G

G#
& D#

Songbook
ONE

Songbook
TWO

Songbook
THREE

Songbook
FOUR

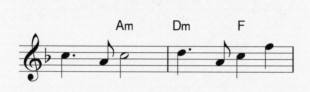

Let The Bulgine Run

Getting
Started

B,A,G

C&D

F#,E,D

Bb&F

Low C
& C#

High
E-G

G#
& D#

Songbook
ONE

Songbook
TWO

Songbook
THREE

Songbook
FOUR

Bound For The Rio Grande

Getting
Started

B,A,G

C&D

F#,E,D

Bb&F

Low C
& C#

High
E-G

G#
& D#

Songbook
ONE

Songbook
TWO

Songbook
THREE

Songbook
FOUR

Getting Started

B,A,G

C&D

F#,E,D

Bb&F

Low C & C#

High E-G

G# & D#

Songbook ONE

Songbook TWO

Songbook THREE

Songbook FOUR

In the Bleak Midwinter

Getting
Started

B,A,G

C&D

F#,E,D

Bb&F

Low C
& C#

High
E-G

G#
& D#

Songbook
ONE

Songbook
TWO

Songbook
THREE

Songbook
FOUR

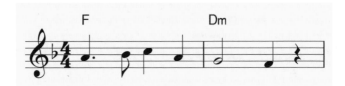

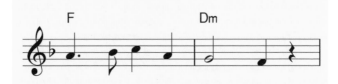

The First Nowell

Getting Started

B,A,G

C&D

F#,E,D

Bb&F

Low C & C#

High E-G

G# & D#

Songbook ONE

Songbook TWO

Songbook THREE

Songbook FOUR

Getting Started

B,A,G

C&D

F#,E,D

Bb&F

Low C & C#

High E-G

G# & D#

Songbook ONE

Songbook TWO

Songbook THREE

Songbook FOUR

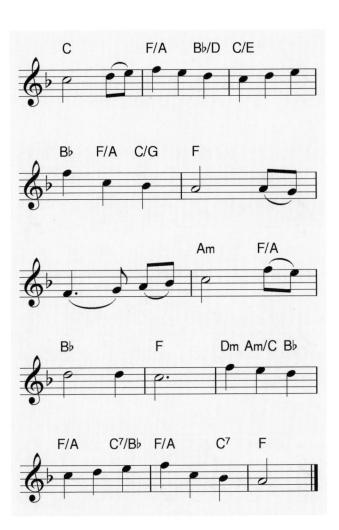

Rocking

Getting
Started

B,A,G

C&D

F#,E,D

Bb&F

Low C
& C#

High
E-G

G#
& D#

Songbook
ONE

Songbook
TWO

Songbook
THREE

Songbook
FOUR

Getting Started

B,A,G

C & D

F#,E,D

Bb & F

Low C & C#

High E-G

G# & D#

Songbook ONE

Songbook TWO

Songbook THREE

Songbook FOUR

The Sussex Carol

Getting Started

B,A,G

C&D

F#,E,D

Bb&F

Low C & C#

High E-G

G# & D#

Songbook ONE

Songbook TWO

Songbook THREE

Songbook FOUR

Getting Started

B,A,G

C&D

F#,E,D

Bb&F

Low C & C#

High E-G

G# & D#

Songbook ONE

Songbook TWO

Songbook THREE

Songbook FOUR

O Come All Ye Faithful

Getting Started

B,A,G

C&D

F#,E,D

Bb&F

Low C & C#

High E-G

G# & D#

Songbook ONE

Songbook TWO

Songbook THREE

Songbook FOUR

Getting Started

B,A,G

C&D

F#,E,D

Bb&F

Low C & C#

High E-G

G# & D#

Songbook ONE

Songbook TWO

Songbook THREE

Songbook FOUR

God Rest Ye Merry, Gentlemen

Getting Started

B,A,G

C & D

F#,E,D

Bb & F

Low C & C#

High E-G

G# & D#

Songbook ONE

Songbook TWO

Songbook THREE

Songbook FOUR

Getting Started

B,A,G

C&D

F#,E,D

Bb&F

Low C & C#

High E-G

G# & D#

Songbook ONE

Songbook TWO

Songbook THREE

Songbook FOUR

Angels From The Realms Of Glory

Getting Started

B,A,G

C&D

F#,E,D

Bb&F

Low C & C#

High E-G

G# & D#

Songbook ONE

Songbook TWO

Songbook THREE

Songbook FOUR

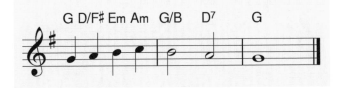

Getting Started

B,A,G

C & D

F#,E,D

Bb & F

Low C & C#

High E-G

G# & D#

Songbook ONE

Songbook TWO

Songbook THREE

Songbook FOUR

Good King Wenceslas

Getting Started

B,A,G

C&D

F#,E,D

Bb&F

Low C & C#

High E-G

G# & D#

Songbook ONE

Songbook TWO

Songbook THREE

Songbook FOUR

Getting Started

B,A,G

C & D

F#,E,D

Bb & F

Low C & C#

High E-G

G# & D#

Songbook ONE

Songbook TWO

Songbook THREE

Songbook FOUR

While Shepherds Watched

Getting Started

B,A,G

C & D

F#,E,D

Bb & F

Low C & C#

High E-G

G# & D#

Songbook ONE

Songbook TWO

Songbook THREE

Songbook FOUR

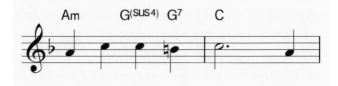

Getting
Started

B,A,G

C&D

F#,E,D

Bb&F

Low C
& C#

High
E-G

G#
& D#

Songbook
ONE

Songbook
TWO

Songbook
THREE

Songbook
FOUR

It Came Upon A Midnight Clear

Joy To The World

Getting Started

B,A,G

C&D

F#,E,D

Bb&F

Low C & C#

High E-G

G# & D#

Songbook ONE

Songbook TWO

Songbook THREE

Songbook FOUR

Getting Started

B,A,G

C&D

F#,E,D

Bb&F

Low C & C#

High E-G

G# & D#

Songbook ONE

Songbook TWO

Songbook THREE

Songbook FOUR

The Coventry Carol

Getting Started

B,A,G

C&D

F#,E,D

Bb&F

Low C & C#

High E-G

G# & D#

Songbook ONE

Songbook TWO

Songbook THREE

Songbook FOUR

Ding Dong Merrily On High

Getting Started

B,A,G

C&D

F#,E,D

Bb&F

Low C & C#

High E-G

G# & D#

Songbook ONE

Songbook TWO

Songbook THREE

Songbook FOUR

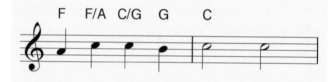

Getting Started

B,A,G

C&D

F#,E,D

Bb&F

Low C & C#

High E-G

G# & D#

Songbook ONE

Songbook TWO

Songbook THREE

Songbook FOUR

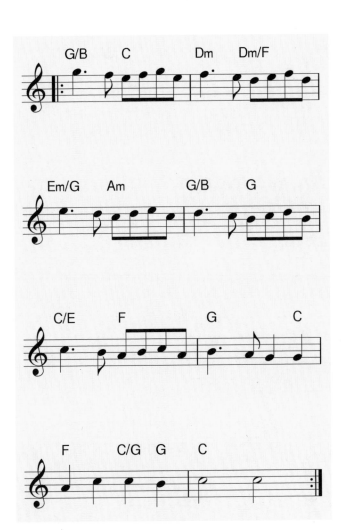

Hark, The Herald Angels Sing

Getting Started

B,A,G

C&D

F#,E,D

Bb&F

Low C & C#

High E-G

G# & D#

Songbook ONE

Songbook TWO

Songbook THREE

Songbook FOUR

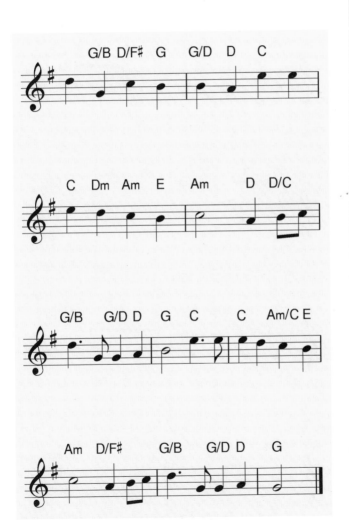

Getting Started

B,A,G

C&D

F#,E,D

Bb&F

Low C & C#

High E-G

G# & D#

Songbook ONE

Songbook TWO

Songbook THREE

Songbook FOUR

Oh Little Town
Of Bethlehem

Once In Royal David's City

The Holly And The Ivy

Getting Started

B,A,G

C&D

F#,E,D

Bb&F

Low C & C#

High E-G

G# & D#

Songbook ONE

Songbook TWO

Songbook THREE

Songbook FOUR

Getting Started

B,A,G

C&D

F#,E,D

Bb&F

Low C & C#

High E-G

G# & D#

Songbook ONE

Songbook TWO

Songbook THREE

Songbook FOUR

331

Silent Night

Getting Started

B,A,G

C&D

F#,E,D

Bb&F

Low C & C#

High E-G

G# & D#

Songbook ONE

Songbook TWO

Songbook THREE

Songbook FOUR

Getting Started

B,A,G

C&D

F#,E,D

Bb&F

Low C & C#

High E-G

G# & D#

Songbook ONE

Songbook TWO

Songbook THREE

Songbook FOUR

Camptown Races

Getting Started

B,A,G

C&D

F#,E,D

Bb&F

Low C & C#

High E-G

G# & D#

Songbook ONE

Songbook TWO

Songbook THREE

Songbook FOUR

Getting
Started

B,A,G

C&D

F#,E,D

Bb&F

Low C
& C#

High
E-G

G#
& D#

Songbook
ONE

Songbook
TWO

Songbook
THREE

Songbook
FOUR

Nelly Was A Lady

Getting Started

B,A,G

C&D

F#,E,D

Bb&F

Low C & C#

High E–G

G# & D#

Songbook ONE

Songbook TWO

Songbook THREE

Songbook FOUR

Getting Started

B,A,G

C&D

F#,E,D

Bb&F

Low C & C#

High E-G

G# & D#

Songbook ONE

Songbook TWO

Songbook THREE

Songbook FOUR

Oh Suzannah

Getting Started

B,A,G

C&D

F#,E,D

Bb&F

Low C & C#

High E-G

G# & D#

Songbook ONE

Songbook TWO

Songbook THREE

Songbook FOUR

I Dream of Jeannie With The Light Brown Hair

Getting Started

B,A,G

C&D

F#,E,D

Bb&F

Low C & C#

High E-G

G# & D#

Songbook ONE

Songbook TWO

Songbook THREE

Songbook FOUR

Old Folks At Home

Getting
Started

B,A,G

C&D

F#,E,D

Bb&F

Low C
& C#

High
E-G

G#
& D#

Songbook
ONE

Songbook
TWO

Songbook
THREE

Songbook
FOUR

Getting Started

B,A,G

C&D

F#,E,D

Bb&F

Low C & C#

High E–G

G# & D#

Songbook ONE

Songbook TWO

Songbook THREE

Songbook FOUR

343

My Old Kentucky Home

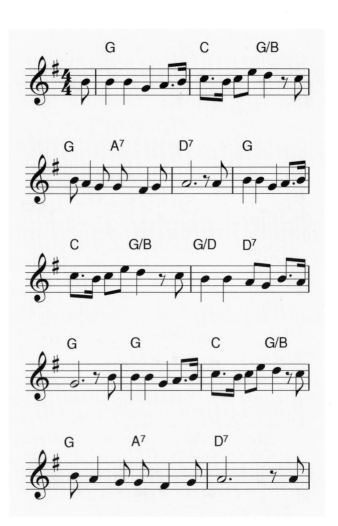

Getting Started

B,A,G

C&D

F#,E,D

Bb&F

Low C & C#

High E-G

G# & D#

Songbook ONE

Songbook TWO

Songbook THREE

Songbook FOUR

345

Getting
Started

B,A,G

C♦D

F#,E,D

Bb♦F

Low C
♦ C#

High
E-G

G#
♦ D#

Songbook
ONE

Songbook
TWO

Songbook
THREE

Songbook
FOUR

Beautiful Dreamer

9/8 is like 6/8, only with three slow beats in each bar.

Getting
Started

B,A,G

C&D

F#,E,D

Bb&F

Low C
& C#

High
E-G

G#
& D#

Songbook
ONE

Songbook
TWO

Songbook
THREE

Songbook
FOUR

Greensleeves

Getting Started

B,A,G

C & D

F#,E,D

Bb & F

Low C & C#

High E-G

G# & D#

Songbook ONE

Songbook TWO

Songbook THREE

Songbook FOUR

Getting Started

B,A,G

C&D

F#,E,D

Bb&F

Low C & C#

High E-G

G# & D#

Songbook ONE

Songbook TWO

Songbook THREE

Songbook FOUR

Air (Handel)

Getting
Started

B,A,G

C&D

F#,E,D

Bb&F

Low C
& C#

High
E-G

G#
& D#

Songbook
ONE

Songbook
TWO

Songbook
THREE

Songbook
FOUR

Morning (Grieg)

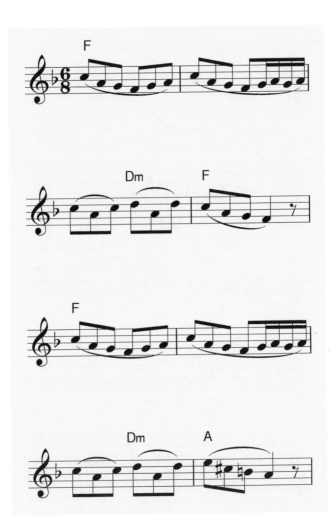

Getting Started

B,A,G

C&D

F#,E,D

Bb&F

Low C & C#

High E-G

G# & D#

Songbook ONE

Songbook TWO

Songbook THREE

Songbook FOUR

Hornpipe (Handel)

Getting
Started

B,A,G

C&D

F#,E,D

Bb&F

Low C
& C#

High
E-G

G#
& D#

Songbook
ONE

Songbook
TWO

Songbook
THREE

Songbook
FOUR

Getting
Started

B,A,G

C & D

F#,E,D

Bb & F

Low C
& C#

High
E–G

G#
& D#

Songbook
ONE

Songbook
TWO

Songbook
THREE

Songbook
FOUR

Bourre (Handel)

This is a long tune, so it has been slightly shortened.

Getting
Started

B,A,G

C&D

F#,E,D

Bb&F

Low C
& C#

High
E-G

G#
& D#

Songbook
ONE

Songbook
TWO

Songbook
THREE

Songbook
FOUR

In the Hall Of The Mountain King (Grieg)

The accompaniment is single bass notes, not chords.

Getting Started

B,A,G

C&D

F#,E,D

Bb&F

Low C & C#

High E-G

G# & D#

Songbook ONE

Songbook TWO

Songbook THREE

Songbook FOUR

Getting Started

B,A,G

C&D

F#,E,D

Bb&F

Low C & C#

High E-G

G# & D#

Songbook ONE

Songbook TWO

Songbook THREE

Songbook FOUR

Fairest Isle (Purcell)

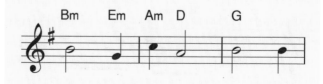

Getting
Started

B,A,G

C&D

F#,E,D

Bb&F

Low C
& C#

High
E–G

G#
& D#

Songbook
ONE

Songbook
TWO

Songbook
THREE

Songbook
FOUR

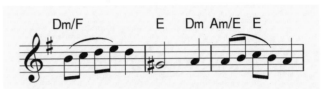

Cradle Song (Brahms)

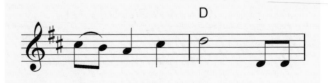

Getting
Started

B,A,G

C&D

F#,E,D

Bb&F

Low C
& C#

High
E-G

G#
& D#

Songbook
ONE

Songbook
TWO

Songbook
THREE

Songbook
FOUR

Pavane

This tune and the next are two old dance tunes
used by Peter Warlock in his suite Capriol; Pavane
is stately, while Basse–Dance is brisk.

Getting Started

B,A,G

C&D

F#,E,D

Bb&F

Low C & C#

High E–G

G# & D#

Songbook ONE

Songbook TWO

Songbook THREE

Songbook FOUR

Basse-Dance

Getting Started

B,A,G

C&D

F#,E,D

Bb&F

Low C & C#

High E-G

G# & D#

Songbook ONE

Songbook TWO

Songbook THREE

Songbook FOUR

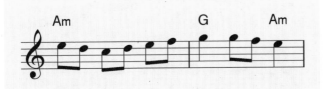

Eine Kleine Nachtmusik
(Mozart)

Getting Started

B,A,G

C&D

F#,E,D

Bb&F

Low C & C#

High E-G

G# & D#

Songbook ONE

Songbook TWO

Songbook THREE

Songbook FOUR

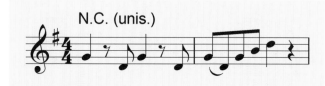

Getting Started

B,A,G

C&D

F#,E,D

Bb&F

Low C & C#

High E-G

G# & D#

Songbook ONE

Songbook TWO

Songbook THREE

Songbook FOUR

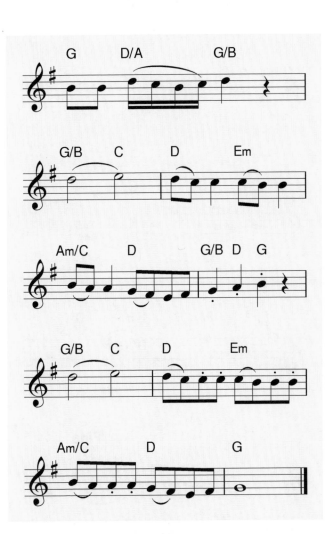

Wedding March
(Mendelssohn)

Getting
Started

B,A,G

C&D

F#,E,D

Bb&F

Low C
& C#

High
E-G

G#
& D#

Songbook
ONE

Songbook
TWO

Songbook
THREE

Songbook
FOUR

Land of Hope and Glory
(Elgar)

Getting Started

B,A,G

C&D

F#,E,D

Bb&F

Low C & C#

High E–G

G# & D#

Songbook ONE

Songbook TWO

Songbook THREE

Songbook FOUR

Getting Started

B,A,G

C&D

F#,E,D

Bb&F

Low C & C#

High E-G

G# & D#

Songbook ONE

Songbook TWO

Songbook THREE

Songbook FOUR

Toreador Song
(Bizet)

Getting
Started

B,A,G

C&D

F#,E,D

Bb&F

Low C
& C#

High
E-G

G#
& D#

Songbook
ONE

Songbook
TWO

Songbook
THREE

Songbook
FOUR

Getting Started

B,A,G

C&D

F#,E,D

Bb&F

Low C & C#

High E-G

G# & D#

Songbook ONE

Songbook TWO

Songbook THREE

Songbook FOUR

Sleeping Beauty Waltz
(Tchaikovsky)

Getting Started

B,A,G

C&D

F#,E,D

Bb&F

Low C & C#

High E-G

G# & D#

Songbook ONE

Songbook TWO

Songbook THREE

Songbook FOUR

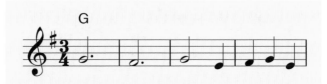

Getting Started

B,A,G

C & D

F#,E,D

Bb & F

Low C & C#

High E-G

G# & D#

Songbook ONE

Songbook TWO

Songbook THREE

Songbook FOUR

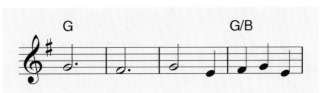

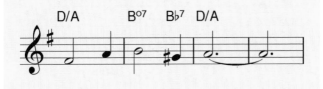

Rabble Rouser

Getting Started

B,A,G

C♦D

F#,E,D

Bb♦F

Low C ♦ C#

High E-G

G# ♦ D#

Songbook ONE

Songbook TWO

Songbook THREE

Songbook FOUR

Waltz Blue

Getting Started

B,A,G

C & D

F#,E,D

Bb & F

Low C & C#

High E-G

G# & D#

Songbook ONE

Songbook TWO

Songbook THREE

Songbook FOUR

Getting Started

B,A,G

C & D

F#,E,D

Bb & F

Low C & C#

High E–G

G# & D#

Songbook ONE

Songbook TWO

Songbook THREE

Songbook FOUR

Reflections

Getting
Started

B,A,G

C & D

F#,E,D

Bb & F

Low C
& C#

High
E-G

G#
& D#

Songbook
ONE

Songbook
TWO

Songbook
THREE

Songbook
FOUR

Slowing

Funky Finale

Getting Started

B,A,G

C&D

F#,E,D

Bb&F

Low C & C#

High E–G

G# & D#

Songbook ONE

Songbook TWO

Songbook THREE

Songbook FOUR

Further Reading

Bay, W., *Recorder Tune Book*,
Mel Bay Publications Inc., 2006

Bush, R. & Bentley, R., *Abracadabra Recorder*,
A & C Black Publishing, 1984

Charlton, A., *How To Read Music*,
Flame Tree Publishing, 2008

Day, H. & Pilhofer, M., *Music Theory For Dummies*,
John Wiley & Sons, 2007

Hawthorn, P. & Hooper, C., *First Book of the Recorder*,
Usborne Publishing, 1997

Hawthorn, P. & Tyler, J., *Easy Recorder Tunes*,
Usborne Publishing, 1990

Lowenkron, S., *Recorder for Beginners*,
Alfred Publishing, 2001

Marks, A., *Very Easy Recorder Tunes*,
Usborne Publishing, 2003

Pitts, J., *Recorder From The Beginning*,
Omnibus Press, 1999

Internet Sites

www.bbc.co.uk/dna/h2g2/alabaster/A506387
www.howto.co.uk/learning/how-read-music/